# DARKWALKER 2
# INFERNO

This is a work of fiction.
Similarities to persons, living or dead,
are neither intended
nor should be inferred.

ISBN: 0-9983882-6-2
ISBN-13: 978-0-9983882-6-7 (DarkFluidity)

# ALSO BY JOHN URBANCIK

## NOVELS
Sins of Blood and Stone
Breath of the Moon
Once Upon a Time in Midnight
Stale Reality
The Corpse and the Girl from Miami
DarkWalker 1: Hunting Grounds

## NOVELLAS
A Game of Colors
The Rise and Fall of Babylon (with Brian Keene)
Wings of the Butterfly
House of Shadow and Ash
Necropolis
Quicksilver
Beneath Midnight
Zombies vs. Aliens vs. Robots vs. Cowboys vs. Ninja vs.
Investment Bankers vs. Green Berets
Colette and the Tiger

## COLLECTIONS
Shadows, Legends & Secrets
Sound and Vision
Tales of the Fantastic and the Phantasmagoric

## INKSTAINS
Multiple volumes

# DARKWALKER 2
# INFERNO

# JOHN URBANCIK

# PART I
# CROSSROADS

1.

He's chasing a ghost. He knows it. He just doesn't give a shit.

Jack Harlow walks into the bar like he owns it, and no one makes any effort to tell him otherwise. There's a band, something jazzy, not entirely his taste but not bad. The bartender's cute, if you like the type.

Once upon a time, not very long ago, he would hide in the shadows. He bought drink after drink in an attempt to drown away the things he sees.

He counts quickly. Three shape shifters, a pack of sorts, not wolves and not of any interest. One vampire, almost as young as he pretends to be, as yet oblivious that he might be watched. But not tonight—not by Jack. He wants someone a bit less substantial.

"Are you back already?" the ghost asks.

Jack says nothing. He walks between the dance floor and the bar, into the kitchen, where the cook gives him nothing more than a glance, and into the cellar.

The steps are narrow, dank and dark and generally disused. They store wine here, and some foodstuffs, the type you forget about until way too late. When the door swings shut, it leaves Jack and the ghost in darkness.

It's okay. Jack sees well through the dark.

He still feels the rhythm from the band. The bass punctuates his pulse. He turns to the ghost, not for the first time, and says, "You're wrong."

"I'm not wrong," the ghost says.

"You don't want to play tricks with me."

The ghost had a name, perhaps retains it, but Jack doesn't care to use it. He's not here to make friends. It's been three months since he lost the woman he loved, three agonizing months, in which he discovered depths of darkness he never imagined. He developed a talent for locks, which came surprisingly easy, and emptied the whiskey shelves of many a liquor store. He wandered. But he didn't go far. A short walk from this bar would return Jack to her apartment. Someone else lives there now. Someone else took her stuff away.

Her name was Lisa Sparrow. He doesn't want her stuff. He's a DarkWalker, able to see the things most people only see in nightmares, able to talk and, to some degree, threaten. It used to be different, but he's a different man now.

Jack Harlow sees a great many things, things of night and shadow and dark, things that never existed, things that never should have. He sees ghosts and revenants and spirits, phantoms and apparitions and specters, visions and visitors, phantasms and haunts and eidolons and shades and echoes, but he cannot see Lisa.

She's dead because of him. He wants to bring her back.

"Why do you stay?" Jack asks. "Why linger in this place where you're forgotten, where you know no one and no one knows you? Why hang around all these descendants of people you never even knew? You've got no connection."

"Except this place."

"No connection," Jack says again. "You can't talk to the them, or touch them, or anything. You're incorporeal, and will always be."

"Same reason you keep coming back," the ghost tells him.

Jack's talking fast. Words spill past his lips without check, without real meaning. He doesn't even know what he's saying. His head swims. He can't focus properly. It's been like that a while now. He's getting used to it, maybe even revels in it.

One thing the whiskey never did was dull the pain.

"You think you know me," Jack tells it. "You think you know anything. You've been less than a wisp of smoke for sixty years, you're buried two hundred miles away, you've got a granddaughter in New Orleans..."

"You looked me up."

Jack doesn't notice the interruption. "You've got all these other places you could be haunting. Tell me this, oh great and insubstantial spirit thing, *why here and not where you died?*"

The ghost smiles sadly. "Come back when you're sober, we'll talk."

Jack glares. "I'm not drunk." He's not. Not a trace of whiskey on his breath. His blood has no taint of alcohol, though he itches for more. The warmth. The harshness. The never-delivered promise of release.

"You're angry, then."

"Damn right."

"I have no answers for you."

"These are some pretty direct and personal questions," Jack tells the ghost. "Nothing about the meaning of life, or what happens to our souls when we die."

The ghost laughs. Those were the questions Jack's been asking over the past few months. "Okay, sure," the ghost says. "I'll tell you what I know. I died over a hundred miles away, as you know. Was a petty crime, trust me, and not worth such a punishment. I linger because, well, I like it, and I don't know if I have a choice yet, and I'm not sure I want to see what waits for me." Jack lets him speak. "And I'm here, in this place, because before they called it The Precipice, before it was the Downtown Jazz Club, before it was rebuilt as the building it is today, it was my bar."

"Yours?"

"I didn't own it," the ghost says. "Mine, because it was where I went. I was a kid. We were all kids. There was no cellar then, none of this, but there was a girl with eyes like sapphires and lips like poison. It was here, with that poison mouth, that she killed me first, before anyone got a chance to do it with lead. She ripped out a part of me, didn't even know it herself, and left it here, under this cement, under this dirt. I became a man here, died here, and was reborn here, on this spot, in this place. My life changed. And while you see all of those wonderful things you see, all the things of this world and whatever other worlds there are, there's only one thing I see. *Eyes like sapphires.*"

The ghost dims, and he smiles, and his focus shifts to memories. He's drifting.

Jack reaches out, touches an arm he cannot really touch, though he feels it and the air beneath it, but has nothing to say. His anger's diluted itself, at least for the moment.

The ghost holds himself present a moment longer. "This place, this Precipice as you call it now, is my crossroads. And when I've had enough of lips like poison and memories, when I no longer see her in every twenty-two year old girl who walks into this place— when I'm brave enough to go on, I'll go."

The ghost fades.

Jack sighs. Closes his eyes. Leans against the wall long enough to feel the cold concrete seep into his skin. His pulse slows, and eventually he no longer feels the vibrations of the bass on stage.

Someone knocks on the cellar door.

Jack's exhausted his rage and his fear and his sorrow. He doesn't know if there's anything left to feel. He wants to bark something rude, but the desire's not really that strong. A woman opens the door, only enough to peek in, to set her blue eyes on Jack, and says, "There's someone looking for you."

Jack blinks at her. Nothing changes, so he blinks again. "What?"

"He says get Jack out of the cellar." The woman smiles. She knows more than she's telling. "He says get Jack out of the cellar, he's ready now. Are you ready now, Mr. Jack? Do you want to talk with someone who might actually be able to help you?"

Jack doesn't bother asking who. He'll find out soon enough.

2.

The woman's blue eyes nearly glow against her deep brown skin. She's not quite human, but it takes a moment for Jack Harlow to realize what she is.

"You're an acolyte."

She smiles. Like the eyes, her white teeth are all contrast. He thinks he recognizes her accent, not just from an island, but a match of someone he met – the vaudoux from Santo Domingo – the night he lost Lisa.

She leads him back into the bar. The band has just begun their next set. The shape shifters and the vampire have gone. The vaudoux commands a corner booth. He's freshly shaven but impossible not to recognize. Even in a black suit and tie, everything is crisp yet somehow tinted tropical. It's more than just the yellow flower in his lapel. omen flank him, two on either side, each a different type of physical perfection. Men sit at the table, too, some who may never have seen the sun the whole length of their lives, only two with skin as dark as the vaudoux. These two are behemoths, unnaturally large, sharp of eye and muscle and dress, lacking the smiles of the women or the other men. A dozen people make up this entourage. Or maybe it's everyone in the bar. Sometimes, it's not always so obvious.

"Sit, please, Mr. Jack," the vaudoux says.

Jack doesn't. The girl with the impossibly blue eyes stays so close, he smells the incense and jasmine and spice of her, and the ocean, and the sand, even the sun. Jack withdraws a silver coin from his pocket. Nothing scars either side.

"You gave this to me."

The vaudoux's smile broadens, if such a thing is possible, and radiates light and hope and trust—none of which are things Jack often associates with the dark. "It was a trade," he says.

"For what?"

"Someday, perhaps, but not today," the vaudoux says. "I want to tell you a story. Please, sit down. You are safe here, and I daresay protected better than anything I could provide."

Jack glances at the acolyte. Besides the vaudoux himself, she's the most dangerous here. He thinks he should distrust her but he doesn't. Not yet.

Finally, Jack Harlow relents and takes the last spot in the booth. The acolyte sits on the edge beside him, her back pressed against his side as she watches the band. Despite the music, there's no need to raise their voices. They can be heard.

"It's a true story," the vaudoux says, "or it was true when it happened, if it ever did. Do you understand?"

"You've been watching me these past three months," Jack realizes. He'd been watching Jack the night he lost Lisa; the vaudoux had watched, but had not interfered—and had not assisted. "Haven't been able to ignore me, have you?"

"I admit, you have a certain fascination."

"You called me friend once."

One of the girls at his side leans close, whispers the vaudoux's his ear, tries not to look at Jack.

"If you meant to kill me, enslave me, make me your zombie, whatever it is you do," Jack says, "you would've already done it. So you want something else."

"I want nothing," the vaudoux says, leaning forward and lowering his voice to something more intoxicating, "but to keep on walking. Tonight, I leave this city. It bores me."

Jack doesn't interrupt.

"A southern wind grows at your back," the vaudoux tells Jack. "I have walked ten thousand miles. We are guided, you and I, and others like us. When we listen, there's no need for questions. The ghost here, the pale reflection of the memory of a man long dead, can no more answer questions about why he is that way than you can answer about yourself."

He leans back, takes a leisurely sip from his glass of rum, and says, "The story, Mr. Jack. It's short. It happens at three in the morning in a city, any city, very possible this city, though I cannot say for certain. A man sells his soul, or believes he sells his soul, for something—say a talent, or a love—it's often something so fleeting as love that leads men to such great sacrifice. But it's not a devil to whom he sells his soul, no demon, but a trickster. A master trickster. The man neither gains what he seeks nor loses what he is prepared to give up. He gets cold, perhaps, a preternatural chill to freeze the marrow in his bones. There may be four points on the compass, four roads to follow, but none is correct and none is wrong."

The acolyte leans back, whispers to Jack, "Listen to what he says. This is the best part."

The vaudoux takes another drink before continuing, but adds nothing more. He merely smiles.

"If you're trying to scare me," Jack says, "you need something a little more concrete."

"I care nothing for fear," the vaudoux says. "And I can inspire none in you, Mr. Jack. You're not invulnerable, but you remain untouchable."

"You think that will change." Once, it had changed; Jack suspects it will change again. The dark cannot touch him anymore than he can touch it. But nothing lasts forever.

The vaudoux merely smiles. "I'm willing to give you something."

"Trade, you mean," Jack says. "Sell."

"*Give*." No trace of the vaudoux's smile remains. "English may not be my native tongue, but I know how to use it."

"Why give me anything?" Jack asks.

The vaudoux leans back, spreads his arms across the back of the booth, and laughs. The girls around him, as one, draw closer to him. Only the acolyte, and Jack himself, do not appear to shift. It's the type of laugh you expect from the islands. "I am no devil, Mr. Jack, and I have no interest in your soul. But I do have interests, so I will perhaps ask a favor of you. A small thing only, which is well within your ability to provide."

Jack wants to lean back, but the black woman with the blue eyes is too close, her skin too warm. Jack can find no comfortable middle between them.

"My friend here." The vaudoux indicates the acolyte with a wave of his hand. "Naomi wishes to travel. To see things I cannot show her." Jack glances at the acolyte called Naomi. She smiles subtly, with neither apology nor seduction. "Show her something."

"Anything in particular?"

He shrugs.

"If I do this," Jack says. He doesn't want to, though his instincts are too raw, unable to scream any warning at him. "If I take her somewhere, show her something, what do I get in return?"

"Besides her company and aid?" The vaudoux shakes his head. "You are a cruel man, Jack Harlow. Remember, as you become harder and crueler in age, that I saw it first. What I will give you, Mr. Jack, is information. Answers. More particularly, one answer, to one question, which burns your breast even now."

Jack moves his mouth, but finds no words.

"You pester ghosts and phantasms," the vaudoux says, "who cannot tell you of roads they have not traveled. The deceased, when they cross, go by their crossroads."

"*Their* crossroads?"

"Every man, woman, and child has a place on this earth, a place special to them and perhaps no one else, where they made a choice, or learned a lesson, or discovered a secret, where they might have gone one way but went another, a physical place where they can honestly say their life changed fundamentally. I'm not talking of love, Jack Harlow, or fear, not necessarily. I speak of paradigm shifts, grand epiphanies, absolute changes in direction."

The vaudoux leans forward, captures Jack's gaze with his intensity, with the brilliant, phosphorescent whites of his eyes, with the deepest, darkest black pit pupils, and lowers his voice so no one anywhere, living or dead, can possibly overhear. "Yours is in a basement."

3.

Jack's been in a basement or two. He likes to think they're all dank, dingy places, cavities, bowels of whatever structure they pretend to support. Three months ago, he killed a thing in a basement, but that was no *crossroads*, not for his life.

It's clear, quite suddenly, once he's heard the vaudoux's suggestion.

He can call it the first basement: the night of his seventeenth birthday. The house was abandoned, his friends had beer and cigarettes, and they needed no excuse for a party. It wasn't a haunted house; there were no tales, no faces in the windows, no murderers, no lingering spirits.

Jack knew little of spirits then.

The lantern had died for only a moment, but it wasn't Marie, his girl at the time, who had her arm around him when the light came back. The ghost was translucent, something unreal and insubstantial, barely more than a breath. She'd said, "Wasn't that just *grand?*" and disappeared.

But she kissed him, in that final moment.

Jack still wonders, years later, if that kiss had changed his life, it if it could have been anyone sitting in that basement. Was that what opened his eyes? That was the night he realized the things he could see. That was the night that set him on his path from dark vision to inescapable dark vision. He didn't know then that he was untouchable, or that he was powerless—even prevented—from interfering. He'd learned that later. But the ghost in that basement—she'd ignited all of this.

He leans back, into the acolyte but he doesn't care this time. Her skin is warm, even comfortable compared to the memories. A lot of miles separate him from that basement. A lot of years. He's never even thought of going back.

"If I wanted to find someone who has gone from this place," the vaudoux says, "someone who left no trace of herself, I would search heavens and hells, all the realms on the other side of just such a crossroads."

Lisa. She was gone. Dead. Lost to Jack forever. But maybe he could see her again. Maybe he could find out what happened after. Maybe he could find the one person who ever made him feel like he wasn't just living, but alive.

He'd been looking to ghosts for answers. He'd been wrong.

The vaudoux slides a pair of coins across the table and says, "You may find these helpful, Jack Harlow."

Shiny, brand new American copper – well, copper-plated zinc, but details aren't as important as the suggestions. Freshly minted, still with their new-coin smell.

Jack doesn't touch them. "They're pennies."

"Your powers of observation run to the extremes of the divine and mundane. Yes, they're pennies."

Jack shakes his head. "I won't incur a debt?"

The vaudoux smiles again. "I like you, Jack. You've a healthy sense of distrust. I'll leave the coins, as though I dropped them anywhere. I detach myself from them, now and forever more. They are not mine, never were, and never will be. They're just pennies. Should you find a couple of pennies in the booth of a jazz club, and should you decide to pick up two clean, consequence-free pennies, you may find them useful." He turns to the acolyte, who has become something very much like an extension of the left side of Jack's body. "Should he leave them, Naomi, I hope you have a pocket...or a pouch."

The unsmiling bodyguards on either side of the vaudoux rise first, grunt, and nod a dismissal. The acolyte stands, pulling Jack to his feet. The whole entourage rolls out of the booth and out of the club smoothly as the band's trombone draws out one long, wet burlesque note.

Jack finds himself watching them leave.

Jack finds Naomi the acolyte still beside him. He's given up on comfort. He likes energized. He likes empowered. He's not sure he wants to think about anything. He should just move. Go. Start.

"We're going north, then," Naomi whispers. "Into the snow and cold?"

Into the snow and cold. His past swims before Jack's eyes. He's not sure they're his own memories anymore or stolen images. He wasn't the same person.

But he doesn't have to go home. Doesn't have to see dad or his sister or his mom's grave. He just has to go back to that abandoned house, which has probably been sold once or twice, even reclaimed by a bank, since his birthday. He's not going back to anything, not really. He's going to a place he barely knows.

The place where a ghost first kissed him.

Jack understands, now, why he's developed such a distaste for contact with the things he sees. They all recall the cold, nasty memory of the last day of regular life.

"I hope you like Mustangs," Jack says.

4.

1969 Mach I 428 CJ Fastback. Faded blue. No rust. Four headlights like Hellbound demons. Jack had rebuilt the engine before his mother died. He wonders, now, if he would've seen her again if he'd stuck around.

The Mustang is where he left it. He's never had trouble, expects none, and doesn't look for it, either. It's been sitting in a dirt parking lot near the railroad tracks in sight of the Interstate.

He hasn't really opened it up in months.

He does the gentlemanly thing, opening the passenger door for Naomi, closing it again once she's inside. He slips into the seat like he never left. The wheel seems to form itself to his fingers. He's always wished it wasn't an automatic transmission, but everything works at least as well as expected, mostly better, and he can easily eat up the thousand miles in ten hours or less.

He revs the engine. It's music. It's sex. It's the only past he's been able to hold onto, and the only future he can count on. He's still trapped in the whirlwind of these past three months, but it's ending soon. Jack Harlow's going home. He's going to see Lisa again. She'll make things right.

He can't help the childish grin on his face when he turns to Naomi. She's buckled herself in. She's staring out the window, up toward the clouds. She's counting, though Jack wouldn't bet it's anything in the sky she's tracking.

Since the vaudoux gave him the pennies—Jack's not stupid, he dropped them into his pocket before the door had closed behind the exiting entourage—Naomi hasn't said a word to him. And he's been in his own little world, his thoughts circling that place, that ghost, that kiss.

There was nothing to it. The merest hint of a kiss, a breath, a brush of whispers. He knows nothing about the ghost, never thought he might want to know. He's not sure he wants to know now. There's no going back, no point in changing course. It's the crossroads he's interested in, not the ghost kiss, not the basement itself. He intends to journey into the depths of death and reclaim one woman from its embrace.

"Ready?" he asks.

The acolyte turns her blue eyes on him. They're not natural, but not contacts, either. Changed. They're like his own eyes, seeing things others cannot. Her smile is brilliant. Layers of depth are there, visible just below the surface, shapes drifting below the ocean waves. But covering all that is a glimmer Jack only barely recognizes.

"Actually," she says, "I could use a bottle of water before we go."

Jack almost laughs. He glances at the gas gauge. A little low. "Sure," he says. He's in a giving mood. "Then the highway."

"I cannot wait."

5.

The guy at the gas station tells Naomi to take what she needs, which she proceeds to do: two bottles of water each and a couple of bars of chocolate. And the fuel. She smiles for him as she leaves, and it seems genuine, but she says nothing.

He says, "Anytime." But his voice if faraway, and his eyes focus somewhere else. She's got a little bit of glamour, perhaps; it does nothing but amuse Jack.

In the Mustang and on the Interstate, he remembers the feel of the highway, the knowledge that he's leaving something behind. It's different this time. At the end of this journey is a place he's been—well, it'll lead to a place he's never been. He's not sure he's ever gone *to* anyplace before.

Naomi finishes half a bottle of water almost immediately, then stares out the window. It's too early for the sun to rise, but it's out there, threatening.

One thing about the darkness Jack knows: it doesn't really care if it's dark. Sure, he's not likely to run into a raging vampire at high noon, but there are things unaffected by sunlight. Some things of darkness thrive in it. The acolyte, like Jack Harlow, DarkWalker, moves freely through both day and night.

"You drive like a man driven," she says.

"That's not really funny."

"It's not meant to be." She still stares out the window. "You're aiming for a destination. You don't understand the journey."

When he doesn't answer, she continues: "If you drive faster, we'll get there sooner, and you'll find what you're seeking, yes?"

"Yes."

"Then faster," she says. She's smiling, a little. She's playing with him. He doesn't care anymore. He's got the needle pressed nicely over 100. The Mustang responds as if to his thoughts, traffic's nearly non-existent, and police are as unlikely to notice him as anything else. There are advantages to being immune to the night.

It's strange, sometimes, the things that do and don't notice him. He's spent a lot of time trying to be invisible. Always, some vampire chick strolls by and strokes his arm, the bar's ghost realizes he's got a drinking buddy, someone nods, something grins. Alcohol numbs his senses, but doesn't stop them from coming. And now, since he's been digging for answers, since he's seeking Death itself, there do seem to be a lot more things out there. Watching. Feeding. Stalking and frightening and devouring.

But a cop in a cruiser? Okay, they'll see him, their radar will report his triple digit miles per. But they'll not bother with him. A few months back, a vampire had admitted she felt a natural repulsion when he was near. It burned to touch him.

He glances at the acolyte. She'd sat up against him in the bar. "The dark," he says. "It usually can't touch me. Why can you?"

"I'm not completely of the dark."

"You're of the light?"

"Not completely."

Jack doesn't like games. "What, you're *balance* then?"

"In balance, yes," she says. She offers no further explanation, but says, "It's not comfortable to touch you, Jack Harlow. Even through clothes, when it is not flesh on flesh, you hurt." She puts a hand on his leg, leans close, and whispers, "Not all pain is bad."

He shakes his leg free. "Why are you coming with me, exactly?"

"To learn."

"What do you want to learn?"

"Something I do not already know."

"You think I can teach you?"

"No."

Jack laughs.

"But," she says, "you will, perhaps inadvertently, show me something." She sips her water and returns to the scenery being devoured by the Mustang.

They cross two state lines before sunrise.

The eastern sky, on the left, while Naomi watches it, first shows signs of color—first a spill of indigo, a bit of blue, a very narrow line of green then yellow. Orange and red round out the rainbow, which sits on the horizon like layers of a cake, the purples stretching out into what was night and the reds widening to hold the rest of the colors to the horizon.

Jack Harlow, DarkWalker, has seen many a sunrise, and many a sunset, but he can't say if each is different than any other he's seen. What he can say, with some certainty, is that another day has started, and if it hadn't been winter he knows he could make it back to that house before sunset. The further north they drive, the colder it gets. The brighter the day becomes, the thicker the traffic. He's dropped their speed to almost 70 because there's not enough room to open it up. Near some sort of city, something small, he's got to make a pit stop. Some things can't be helped.

The acolyte yawns as he pulls off the highway. "So soon?" she asks.

"Quick break," he says. The Mustang needs fuel. He'll have to stop again before they reach the house.

The chocolate bar kept him through the night, but maybe they should get a real breakfast, something with eggs and meat and hash browns. Some juice. The kind of breakfast his mom might've made. He misses her. Does she still linger at the house or the graveyard? Will it be possible to see her? Would he find anything to say? He's been closer to home; but now, he's going there, on purpose, and it's different than being a mere fifty miles away. "Breakfast."

"Ah," Naomi says. "Bread, butter, coffee. Any chance of finding a place serving *akasan*?"

Jack shakes his head. "I don't even know what that is."

"It's got cinnamon," Naomi says.

He pulls into the parking lot of a place that can best be called a dive. The walls seem crooked, the paint hangs in peels, but there's smoke rising from a chimney in the back and there's a good, smoky maple aroma surrounding it.

The acolyte follows Jack into the self-proclaimed diner. It's all dark, thick wood, plush cushions, low lighting. The hostess at the door smiles vacantly and says something like, "Table for two?"

"Three," the acolyte says.

Jack hates games. As the hostess leads them to a booth, Jack asks, "Three?"

"It's never good to be caught by surprise and not have an extra seat for a friend."

"I have no friends," he tells her.

The hostess leaves them with two ragged menus. Naomi opens hers up immediately and seems to forget they'd been talking.

No hash browns on the menu, so Jack decides to go with grits. They're not far enough north yet. Day's still young. Three eggs, double order of bacon. Naomi asks for two plates of pancakes.

"Hungry?" Jack asks.

She shrugs.

Their guest arrives just after the food. He grins widely, looks from Naomi to Jack, and starts by picking a piece of bacon from Jack's plate even as he pulls one order of pancakes closer to him.

"It's gonna be one helluva day, don't you think?" he asks, then starts shoveling pancakes into his mouth.

6.

He's a big guy, not someone you'd want to meet in a dark alley. Of course, Jack Harlow meets a lot of people—and things—in dark alleys.

He's big, and he's got one of those cocky grins that beg to be wiped off with some combination of blood and mud. Platinum blond hair out of a Hollywood saloon. Twinkling eyes. Teeth flash white when he smiles, which he does grandly and frequently. He speaks between bites, constantly tossing bits of pancake into his throat. It's obscene, the way he eats.

Sometimes, Jack Harlow, DarkWalker, knows what a thing is. Knowledge comes from a combination of experience, hearsay, and intuition. In this case, the words are on his tongue before he even knows what he's saying. "Scum Sucker."

"You know," the guest says, punctuating it with a stab of pancake, "I never really liked that title."

"You're our guest?" Naomi asks. Because obviously she'd ordered the extra plate for someone. Jack hates not knowing what's going on, but more than that, he hates being kept in the dark.

He's nearly finished his pancakes, and has already stolen a second piece of Jack's bacon. Jack hasn't touched his breakfast; neither, he notices, has the acolyte.

"You expecting the Thorny Prince, perhaps? The ghost of General Sumter hisownself?"

Jack's not willing to play. "Do you want something?"

"This," he says. "That." The Scum Sucker glances at Naomi and adds, "A piece of that, perhaps."

Her voice is little more than a whisper. "You're not welcome here."

"Me?" He laughs. "Not welcome?" There's no sign of amusement in his laughter. "Quite a bit of nerve you've got there, coming into my town, *my* little haunt, and telling *me* I'm not welcome." He shoots his gaze back to Jack. "You gonna let this harlot talk to me like that?"

Jack's fists are clenched beneath the table. "I asked you nicely."

"And I told you nicely," the Scum Sucker says.

"You haven't told me a damn thing."

The Scum Sucker grins. "Oh. Right. Yeah, well, I forget sometimes. Sorry about that." He leans back. "I count seventeen *guests* in this diner. I ain't counting you, or your girl, and I ain't counting me. Suzie, Pete, Chrissy, they're staff. Family, you might say. They're in addition to that seventeen." He takes coffee in gulps between sentences. "There's a girl, about three, she's the youngest, and there's a man of sixty-seven in the parking lot making his way in. Already counted him." The Scum Sucker leans forward, lowers his voice and broadens his grin. "What will you give me not to kill them all?"

7.

First time Jack Harlow met a Scum Sucker was on a subway in New York City. Could've been the same guy. He had the same grin, held his head slightly lopsided, and hung from the handhold like a puppet. It wasn't crowded. Jack was still new at this seeing things, so when the words Scum Sucker came to mind, he'd thought he was merely describing the guy.

The guy had whispered then, so no one but Jack could hear. "Seven passengers." He licked his lips. "I might just kill them all."

The train had stopped. The doors slid open. Jack said, "Have at it," and walked out.

He wonders, now, what became of the seven passengers, if they'd suffered or died quickly or returned to their wives and husbands and children without knowing how close death had come to them.

Death comes by many means. Claw. Tooth. Bullet. Train. *Knife.*

8.

Jack can do the same thing today. He can grab the acolyte by the hand and drag her out of the diner, perhaps leave a tip for the waitress, not cause any commotion, no alarm, nothing to see here.

But Jack's older now. He hasn't breathed New York air in years, and though he doesn't actually know much of anything, he knows a hell of a lot more than he did then.

He knows he's safe. He's the only one. The Scum Sucker won't kill him, won't hurt him, can't even touch him. It's how they are, how the night treats him. Jack's just another shadow, another bit of the night.

He's not completely immune. He's not entirely untouchable. He meets the Scum Sucker's eye, lowers his own voice, and says, "You can't." It's neither plea nor statement of disbelief, but a revelation. There's a moment in which nothing happens and no one moves; you can hear a fly buzzing near the window on the other side of the diner, the sizzle of bacon. The smells of stale grease, bad deodorant, plastic leaves, peeling paint, and things unmentionable and unknowable, become suddenly acute. One of the long fluorescent tubes in the ceiling pops, and briefly the diner's shadows flicker.

The Scum Sucker is weak. Pathetic. Jack doesn't tell him these things with words, but his eyes hold nothing back, and this pseudo-nighttime thing drops back in his chair, sucks in breath through his teeth. It doesn't feed on death. It feeds on dismay, worry and doubt, and it wants Jack to feel these things. Jack refuses.

"Still," the Scum Sucker says, getting up, "one helluva day, ain't that right?" He strolls, with a degree of nonchalance—forced—toward the back, the kitchen or the restroom or, most likely, some hiding place known to no one else.

"I can't eat this," Jack says, pushing his plate toward the table's center and turning his eyes on the acolyte. "Have you got something to tell me?"

"I'm impressed."

"Three plates?"

"You don't always have uninvited guests," she says with a casual shrug. "But you can't expect never to have any."

"You're serious, aren't you?"

She changes the subject. "Why didn't he kill anyone?"

"He feeds on their petty sufferings," Jack says. "Melodramas. Kill them, and he starves."

"You knew this?"

He didn't really know until she asked. He doesn't tell her this, but he now has a little more certainty about what happened on that subway car. "His kind's all talk. He meant to feed on me, my worry and my concern."

"You have no concern then?" she asks. "No compassion?"

Jack offers a brief grin. "I had no reason to worry about *him*."

9.

They don't talk much. Through most of three or four states, she sleeps. She looks pretty and peaceful when she sleeps, and it's a restful sleep, without excessive movements, fitfulness, or mumbling. Jack doesn't think he'll ever sleep that way again.

The drive remains smooth, if interrupted by typical northeast traffic after they pass the capital, until they're on the New Jersey Turnpike.

It's already a mess of a road, construction here and there, tolls, bridges, lanes closed, huge signs telling you how far it is to New York City, structures that look like huge barrels belching smoke into air.

They make a pit stop – toilet and a couple bottles of water, and gas. The gas jockey grins at them through the passenger window, grins mainly at the acolyte who must be turning up her glamour—Jack sees the shimmering of it—and says, "Oh, no, it's on me today. My pleasure."

"Have you ever paid for anything in your life?" Jack asks.

She shrugs.

Five minutes after the gas jockey, a shape tumbles toward the Turnpike from the side of the road. At first, Jack thinks it's a normal shadow, a crane or some piece of earth-moving equipment. But it moves toward the highway pretty fast. It doesn't look like it's going to stop. And, getting closer, Jack sees it's not touching the ground. Its wingspan is as wide as the highway, but it casts no shadow. It's a white shape, its feathers the size of men, with a bright red beak and sharp talons. It squawks something awful, like an eagle crossed with a tiger with ten times the bass. The Mustang trembles. It's on an attack run, about to pick prey right off the highway.

But no one sees it.

No car swerves to avoid it, no semi slams on its air horn or brakes. The police car thirty yards ahead of Jack doesn't turn on sirens or flashers. Even the acolyte, staring out the side window, doesn't seem to look at it.

It moves fast. Jack has time to slip into the rightmost lane before the roc—for that's what it is, a giant predatory bird, white but dirty, and apparently invisible to everyone but Jack Harlow —before it strikes.

It veers away from the Mustang at the last moment. Its talons strike the top of a Volkswagen Beetle, one of the new ones, bright red and happy one moment and suddenly crumpled the next. The roc lifts the car at least a meter before dropping it again and flying off. It's rising, circling, preparing for another attack.

Jack pulls his wheel and turns the Mustang sharply off the road. The Volkswagen moves sideways at 60mph. The crack is deafening when it hits another car. Both bounce in opposite directions. The Beetle hits a soccer mom on the left. The other car, a Japanese sedan with little to distinguish its actual make, screeches to a halt half in the shoulder. The SUV immediately behind it doesn't even touch its brakes; it smashes through the Japanese car, throwing it to the side.

All this, of course, Naomi does notice.

Another half dozen cars get involved before Jack sees the shadowless bird aiming for the Beetle again. "It's coming back."

"What's coming back?"

Jack points. "That roc."

Naomi blinks, and her jaw drops. "Is that really something?"

"What do you see?"

"I don't know...a shimmer, a glow, a disturbance, a flash of red." Naomi's squinting, following the roc's path. "Is it a *bird?*"

The roc hits the Beetle again, this time snatching it and holding it. The driver's door, partly open, swings wide. The driver falls fifteen feet. Jack flinches when he lands on the trunk of an old Trans Am.

Naomi also flinches. She probably can't see the Beetle in the roc's clutches, not entirely, not as anything more than a tint of red against the sky.

Another crack sounds when someone, not paying attention, smacks the back of a car in front of them.

"We've got to go," Jack says. He touches the accelerator gently, easing through the shoulder, around the sedan, and back onto the Turnpike in front of the accident. He counts at least nine cars, not including the Beetle. The driver is dead, and it'll be a bitch for anyone to explain where he came from. There's a lot of yelling, and horns, and in another minute no one else will be able to follow Jack's route around it.

"You're not going to help?" Naomi asks.

"How could I help? I see things, I can't control them."

She doesn't answer. She has none to give.

He'd tried, more than once, to do something about the things he sees. The one time he successfully helped someone—Lisa—nearly destroyed him, and he hadn't been able to save her in the end.

"We're almost there," Jack says. "Another couple hours, that's all."

He wonders something, though. Something silly, something small, something for which he'll never find an answer: of all the cars on all the roads, why did the roc target that one?

It's not enough of a question to make him stop. Jack puts the accident behind him. He's overly sensitive, though, as sunset nears. He'd wanted to reach that basement before nightfall.

10.

They don't.

Dusk arrives without incident, painting pink fluff in the skies and long shadows on the roads. Things start to emerge from places Jack Harlow never noticed before. He sees them now, shapes slithering from grates on the bottoms of buildings they pass, or crawling, crouched, along the rooftops. In one alley, a man scratches a sickle moon onto the bricks with chalk, but he's not exactly a man and it's not just a drawing. Faces leer at Jack from rest stops, from buses, from the back and front seats of taxis.

When night falls, so close to New York City, the shadows teem with flitterings and shadows and half-forgotten images of things that might or might not eat a man without reason or even hunger. Jack's more alert than ever, seeing more, hearing howls and growls and chattering and slurping, even with the windows up in the Mustang, even at 80mph.

They pass New York City over a bridge, reaching the Expressway, and less than an hour later, without any real incident, reach the exit.

Nothing's changed.

"This is where you grew up?" the acolyte asks when they've entered a subdivision. There's no traffic to speak of, only a few teenagers hanging out at one of the corners, lights on in at least half the houses—but here and there the streetlamps are dark and the shadows thick.

A few more turns, Jack manages to completely avoid the house where he grew up. It's only a few blocks away. But his mother's dead, his father useless, his sister a mere memory. There are high tension electrical wires strung far above the houses here, a wide clearing through which the energy flows. It's invisible, even to Jack, but he at least imagines he can sense it. Just like back then.

The house in question is alongside the clearing, in the fall zone should someone ever knock over the tower.

"It's where I started," Jack says.

"You don't want to see your old house?"

"Not why I'm here."

Jack pulls the Mustang to the side of the road right under the wires, exactly between the house on the right of the clearing and the house on the left — with the basement.

Someone lives there now. They're not home.

There's a chain link fence, waist high, as though that might prevent anything from getting in or out. The one car driveway is two strips of cement separated by dirt with patches of grass. A lamp is on in the living room, so through the window Jack sees everything: couch, television, the hallway to the bedrooms and the opening to the kitchen. There's no dining room; it's not that big a house. Behind the kitchen, there's a back door and a stairway to the basement. Jack remembers every detail.

They'd gone in through that back door. The glass had already been broken. They'd snuck into the basement, careless of the creaking wooden steps. It was an empty cavern, already filled with the odor of stale cigarette smoke and beer.

"It was my birthday," Jack says, staring at the house. He's still behind the wheel of the Mustang. The engine's still running.

"What did you see?"

He doesn't look at her. Doesn't care what she's doing. He sees the house as it is now and as it was then—the skeleton of the present glimmering over the vibrant past.

"I didn't feel her, though she had her arm around me," Jack says. "I knew she was a ghost, right from the start, before the girls started screaming, before anyone ran."

She'd said, *Wasn't that just grand?* before fading away. Oddly, he felt her disappear, though she'd been no more substantial than a breath of air.

"What was her name?"

"The ghost?" Jack shakes his head. "Never knew."

"You never asked," Naomi says.

"I never do." He's lying. He did ask, once; the ghost had been Claire Winters, and he might never shake her entirely from his mind. He feels guilt. Shame. Sorrow.

Of course, ghosts like to tell him things he never asked.

Jack's tired, excited and nervous, and several flavors of anxious. He even feels hope, however small. His head knows better. He's chasing ghosts, quite literally, and that never ends well.

He lets the Mustang rest and climbs out of the car. Naomi follows. Like partners in a crime noir, they approach the house. Crickets sing. A lonely whippoorwill trills, but it's no omen. It's just a bird.

The gate stands wide, not even pretending at being a barrier. Still, Jack pauses here, touches the cold metal, sees around it to the house that once had no such pretense. The house is smaller than he remembers. It's hard to fit such a strange and powerful memory into reality.

He doesn't go to the front door. He never did, not here. The lock on the back door is simple and flimsy and not merely willing but nearly exuberant to open for him. Naomi acknowledges this ability with a quick little sound which might equally mean *I'm impressed* or *I'm waiting to be impressed*. The platform before the basement door is just big enough for two, and only because all doors open out from it. There's the one to the backyard, one to the kitchen—which is half window covered by light curtains—and there's one to the basement.

Here, Jack doesn't hesitate.

He hears the sounds around the house, the rustlings of squirrels and foxes and feral cats. He thinks nothing of them. He sees shadowy figures, but he sees those everywhere and cannot be bothered. There's even a voice, but it's modern, almost mechanical, and of no concern.

Jack and Naomi descend into the basement.

In his memory, it was empty. Now, boxes line one wall. There's a weight lifting bench, dumbbells, a small boom box and television, and a washer and dryer in the far corner. An oval rug marks the workout area; the rest of the floor is bare concrete. A huge wooden box sits against the wall, something that might have been a bed with four drawers underneath, but cardboard boxes and stacks of books occupy the top. One of the drawers is partly open, revealing stored clothes or linens.

There's no sign of the ghost. Jack didn't expect to see her again.

There's no sign of the crossroads, either, but Jack's not quite sure what to look for. "Where is it?"

"I won't be able to see it," Naomi says. "It's yours, not mine. It means nothing to me and I cannot cross it."

Jack wanders to the center of the basement. There's not a lot of light; it all slips in through the narrow windows lining the ceiling or the television, which had been left on and casts a blue glow upon everything.

Naomi turns off the television.

Jack withdraws the pennies from his pocket. He rubs them between two fingers, absently, almost unaware he's doing it until the scent of copper catches his attention, and the faintest glimmer sparks between them. He lifts the coins to his face, stares at them, slides them back and forth more quickly. It's like trying to start a fire with sticks. There's smoke only he can see. There's a tingling, and a tinkling like a thousand butterflies on a thousand empty champagne glasses, and a brief sense of dizziness.

Jack hears music, blues, perhaps with a steel drum in the faraway background. Voices, too, but the voices are fading even as they descend the stairs into the basement.

"Jack Harlow," the lead voice says, but she's already fading. Naomi, however, reacts quite violently, as though shocked or shot. Three, four, five of them descending the steps, all in uniform, all armed except the woman in the lead, all wearing masks except the woman. He almost recognizes her, and then he's not in the basement at all.

Jack finds himself in Hell.

11.

Some time later, Jack Harlow will return and find the basement empty except for the boxes and the weights, the faint scents of blood and sulfur and ozone, and the shimmering echo of a familiar ghost.

# PART II
# JACK HARLOW IN HELL

1.

It's hot.

Yeah, he expects that. He expects flames and magma and a chorus of screaming, and there's all of that, too.

Jack Harlow stands at the end of a tunnel. It descends in a crooked line, with an uneven floor, to a section of some hellish place that isn't exactly *Hell*, per se, but isn't exactly not. He has trouble fixing the place. There's no *Welcome to the Eighth Level* sign, or anything that might help him, and his own senses are muddled and shifty and uncertain.

He hadn't expected a hell. Lisa shouldn't be suffering. There must be other options—and ways to get there.

The tunnel is carved from orange and red and brown strata, crumbling in places but solid like granite in others. It's a well-traveled path. It leads to a cavernous cathedral. Where stained glass windows would line the sides of a traditional church, the openings here have no glass and show only magma-falls and rising steam, smoke, and ash. People—no, souls—are stuffed into the pews like sardines, chanting in an amalgamation of every language ever known to man and quite a few others. They sway back and forth like worshippers at a Baptist revival camp.

On the altar, flanked by orange-furred hounds with teeth and more teeth, surrounded by naked, hairless altar girls, and adorned in vestments of crimson and gold, a Preacher delivers his homily. He's talking about angels and demons and surfboards and rivers of white-hot magma. He's talking about signs from the Heavens and signs from the Hells. He's talking about determination and perseverance and goal setting. He's talking about winters in Siberia. His congregation numbers in the thousands.

There are no doors, just dozens more caves like the one from which Jack emerges.

Quite suddenly, the chanting stops, all movement ceases, and the sermon comes to an abrupt end. The Preacher looks directly at Jack. The entire mass of souls separating them turn as one to look upon the new arrival.

Unlike the Preacher, their faces are plain, and betray only the slightest hint of human features—shadows which might once have been eyes and mouth—pale, reddened, and darkened by soot.

"There comes a time," the Preacher says, "after untold thousands of lifetimes, that a man comes into your house who brings hope. Even in a hopeless pit like this."

The Preacher grins like a piranha. Licks his lips. Draws a deep breath and screams.

They all scream, ten thousand suffering souls combining to create a sound that would shatter chalkboards and fingernails. It's agony and pain and eternity and helplessness and brimstone wrapped into a single, undulating note. It overwhelms Jack. He can't breathe. He can't stand. Jack falls to his knees, clamping his hands over his ears. Blood fills his eyes and mouth.

The souls rise from the pews. They push and scrabble and scrape and crawl, each trying to get closest to the new arrival, the only living soul in this forsaken cathedral. They'd built it with their own hands, drained all their bodily fluids to make the mortar, used their own body fat and muscle and tissue to make the bricks, until nothing remained of them but stringy husks. They pray and sing and chant with the memory of voice. They hope with the echoes of forgotten hope.

They need more bricks.

But as the Preacher approaches, girls behind him, hounds at his sides, a path amongst the souls parts like a sea. Though they've formed a semicircle around Jack, and though Jack isn't sure he has strength enough to rise from his knees, he holds up his head and stares directly at the Preacher.

"You," the Preacher says, "are a sinner, an outcast, and a burden. You are a leech. You are selfish, immature, and unreasoning. You are a fool. And yet, you are *alive*. Even here, even in this pit, this hellhole, to which no soul comes anymore, from which no soul goes, you are an abomination, a freak of the unnatural, and, for my flock, you are a lesson."

The scream is over. It's been over. Jack's ears still ring. His vision remains blurry. But he meets the Preacher's gaze and says, "I am...no...lesson." Each word is a chore to expel from his throat.

"Delusional and incoherent, too," the Preacher says. "How far can a man fall? Smell the traces of whiskey in his blood, my children. Look at the desperation in his eyes. He comes because he wants to come, straight into the bowels of this pit, this hell, this damnation. He's fallen farther than a living man can fall. Feel the waves of revulsion emanating from him, my children. On the surface, he could be a man to be feared, or awed, or esteemed. He could be a god among mortals, but he chooses to seek love beyond the barriers of death."

The Preacher leans closer, sneering, eyes twinkling, enjoying Jack's weakness and pain. But Jack's recovering already. He reaches out, grabs the Preacher's arm.

"Ah," the Preacher says, and then he sighs. "The souls here have experienced torments beyond your comprehension. Your touch may repel those on the surface, but here, underneath it all, the pain we suffer at your touch is like pleasure." He raises his voice to speak to the souls all around. "Pleasure, my children. A brief respite with merely a touch. Please, now, lay your hands upon this glowing, breathing being. Touch the core of him so that you may remember something of life."

Jack fails to struggle. He tries, but there's no point. The souls surge forward. They draw him into the crowd. Each touches him, without discretion or consideration. Hands feel his face, his neck, his shoulders, his back, his crotch, his legs, his arms. They caress and hold and touch and poke and prod. They lift him into the air like an oversized ragdoll and pass him, over their heads, deeper into the pit. They tear at his clothes, scratch his flesh, and draw blood. There's nothing subtle or seductive or even slightly enjoyable about it. It's violation after violation.

Jack Harlow, untouchable on Earth, cries silently as they pass him along. And the souls, the thousands among the Preacher's congregation, they lick the tears out of his eyes with sandpaper tongues. They have no memory of moisture in a place like this.

It's only a preview. There's more than one hell. Jack didn't know. He didn't know, and now he suffers for it. They twist and bend and crack him. The souls scuffle with each other, but all of them, every one—some more than once—put their near-transparent, near-weightless hands on him, feathery touches in such numbers as to be like needles.

Eventually, after hours or days, they deposit Jack on the altar. The Preacher sits on his throne. The hounds step forward, sniffing, pushing him this way and that with their burning noses. The altar girls, not like the Preacher and not like the souls, approach him with knives. Tiny knives. Small, but probably sharp, these knives are designed to filet the flesh and skin and add to the walls of the cathedral.

"Only a little higher," the Preacher says to his congregation, "and we can ascend. This living thing is the proof of our good work, the reward for our suffering."

2.

Jack Harlow lies on his back. He feels nothing, not anymore. Battered into numbness, he sees the advancing Preacher, the souls, the knives, and Jack makes no move to protect himself. He's always been protected. He shouldn't need to move.

But this is Hell, or some variation. Things here work differently. It's something he'll have to remember, should he be able to retain memories.

And there: the loss of memory inspires a twitch of fear.

The first blade cuts into his arm. Pain. Pain and fear together. Self-preservation.

This isn't what he seeks. He came looking for Lisa on the other side—but not in a place like this.

The pennies are still in his pocket. He reaches them, despite the cuts, despite the knives, despite the chanting that draws blood from his ears. He touches them, rubs them together with the barest bit of will—there's no strength to be found. He says nothing, not even when the Preacher scowls, not even when the Preacher fades, not even when the souls cry out in united agony.

The sound lingers in Jack's ears. He rolls over, just slightly, pain erupting with every movement.

It's cooler here. Or he can't feel the heat anymore. It's darker, too, no bright reds or oranges, something gray and ashen, but Jack's eyes fail. He drops his head to the soft ground and slips out of consciousness.

3.

Over the days that follow, the months, the years, Jack doesn't move. He breathes so shallowly, he might be mistaken for dead. There's warmth in his blood, yes, but it's coagulating, slowing, doing only the least necessary to keep him on this side of death, even whilst he lays in the dust of another hell.

Jack's eyes blink open, briefly, then close again for another long time. Only gray surrounds him. Not darkness. Shapes near and far. The chorus of souls has fallen silent. The ground is cool beneath his cheek, dry but spongy.

At first, he cannot move.

Jack opens his eyes again. Spiders crawl across him, weaving their thick webs. He's been covered, pinned to the ground. Aware now, he feels the eight-footed things crawling all over him—two or three dozen — crisscrossing each other, securing their catch.

None has bitten him yet, at least not that he feels.

He blinks again, but the effort only scrapes his eyes. There's no moisture left. His lips aren't chapped, they're cracked like the floor of Death Valley.

He pushes himself up, putting all his frail strength into it, struggling, sweating drily, and with a certain degree of pain. His tongue tastes of sandpaper. His lips are raw but there's not a drop of blood to bleed.

The spiders pause, en masse, as the first of their webs, and perhaps a second, strains and breaks. Then they scatter. They make no sound, but Jack feels every individual foot on his skin. The spiders abandon him as he rises, snapping strands of silk.

He's in the middle of a street, or a plain, something level and solid. There's a layer of soft gray beneath him.

Ash. But it's no mere layer; it's thick and springy and reaches deeper than Jack can understand. He crawls, because walking is too much a risk, toward the nearest structure. There are hundreds, scattered to the horizon in every direction, as gray as the ash beneath him and no less dusty.

He reaches the first of the ruins. Nothing stands straight or tall. Everything leans or sags; everything has the distinct powdery look of the ground. Jack climbs to his knees, still unstable, and reaches for the doorknob. It crumbles at his touch. It falls away in flakes, then the entire building with it. Though there's no wind, the flakes of pure decay flutter and drift.

Each flake, Jack realizes, was once a soul, the remnant of something that had lived, something that had breathed and loved and struggled and died. No consciousness remains, no memory, not a hint of form or function. Only the spiders live here. Within the structure, now disturbed, there is a nest, a massive nest, from which a thousand tiny spiders emerge. They scuttle in every direction, ignoring Jack Harlow, walking over him if he happens to be in their way.

Again, as in the cathedral, they have no fear of him. They touch him at will.

Jack Harlow, in another level of hell, accepts that he came without protection, without weapons, without foresight or a plan. Blinded by desire. By hope. By a skewed sense of fairness.

He sighs. He sleeps. He wakes, he turns, he brushes the spiders away, and he sleeps again. It's neither cold nor hot here. Neither light nor dark. The sky is as a gray as the ground, the horizon indeterminable. Jack needs water. He needs to work his muscles before they atrophy. He needs to get out of hell, and he has no Monopoly card that says *Get out of hell free.*

Eventually, he knows, he has to take out the pennies, rub them, find another level of hell, then another and another until he finds a way out. He never asked. He never questioned. He never *thought.*

He spends days counting the spiders, naming them, trying to understand their purpose. At two thousand, he gives up counting. He's out of names. They merely walk across this ashen terrain.

When one of the other ashen buildings falls, without a sound, Jack knows. The spiders, with their weightless footfalls, tamp down the ash and level the fields. They are the final scourers, doing their bit to remove all vestiges of everything. He checks his skin for signs of gray, but there is only the infernal dryness, the cracking, the vanishing scars from a hundred tiny cuts.

"I can't stay here forever," Jack says aloud. His words are dusty, his throat unused to making sound.

It's quite a statement. He has little with which to back it up. Jack stands, unsteadily, with a degree of uncertainty on the unstable ashen ground.

A moment later, or an hour, as time is all aflutter and it's impossible to be sure of anything anymore, there's a ripping sound, then a crunching, and heavy thunderous roiling. All around, ash structures are collapsing without the slightest noise, sending puffs of dust in all directions. The spiders run, all in a single direction, and disappear through little rips in the fabric of hell. He turns to see what they're fleeing.

4.

The somber grays are giving way to oozing magma and blazing, three-story tall spider-like mechanicals lugging bricks the size of bridges. A legion of orange and red colored stick figures move with the molten earth, before and after it, within it, and climb across the machines like arachnids from hell—an idea which, Jack realizes, is entirely supported by the situation.

One of the stick figures is next to him. It arrived soundlessly, as though it had always been there. It wears a hardhat and carries a clipboard.

The thing consults its clipboard. At first, Jack isn't sure what these stick figures are called; even close up, it's rail thin and lanky with sharp joints at the elbow, wrist, and knee. It looks at Jack, though its face is little more than a smudge of orange. It stands a head shorter than Jack, and at first seems to have no facial features at all. Two dark smudges indicate where eyes might be, and a narrow slash marks a mouth.

The Infernal Crewman speaks as though it's never used voice before, and the slash mouth rips open anew to form each word. "Who are you?" it asks. "What are you doing here?"

"I'm Jack," he says. "Who are you?"

The Crewman ignores the question, flips a few pages back and forth on his clipboard, and finally lowers it. "What's your title?"

Jack gives it some thought. Does he have a title? He's not sure. It's hard to be sure of anything anymore. He's losing his grip on his memories on this ashen, spider-filled plateau. He has to hold on to something, anything, any part of himself, more than just his name. A title might do quite nicely. "DarkWalker."

"Quite a title," the Crewman says. "Everywhere you go, there's another prince of that, a lord of this, dukes and earls, counts and duchesses, barons, marquees, caliphs, popes, khans, tsars, and fuhrers. It gets tiresome. But never, to my recollection, a DarkWalker. That's something unique, is it not?"

Jack hesitates. "I suppose."

"Great," the Crewman says, looking again at the clipboard. "Then you're not *Toge no ouji*. Great. That's settled." The thing pulls a stick-made walkie-talkie out of its stick body, presses a button, and says, "Foreman."

The response is quick and sharp, tinny, crackly, but still a deeply resonant voice. "Crewman."

"One stray...something," the Crewman says. "I say we're good to go. Level all of it and everything, pave over it, run through the lava, and erect one infernal tower."

The Foreman sounds excessively satisfied over the radio. "Good."

The Crewman shoves the stick back into itself and starts to walk away from Jack.

"Wait," Jack says, grabbing its arm. The contact burns, and the stick arm is sharp enough to slice ribbons into Jack's hand. He pulls it back before the Crewman can even respond.

"I have no business with you," the Crewman says. "We have a Hell to erect." Indeed, the machines come closer at an amazing pace, barreling through the ash and leaving rock and stone and orange sky in their wake. A few more minutes, they'll roll right over Jack Harlow. The other Crewmen crawl over everything with claw hammers and heavy sledges. Behind them, Zookeepers with flaming whips and cat-o-nine tails lead a series of chained Souls into this newly forming realm.

Whatever hell had been here before, it's served its purpose. The remnants, barely flakes of ash, hardly able to stand together, had been beaten into smaller and smaller pieces by the march of a million spiders to make way for a newer hell. Jack had never imagined hells were recycled.

The new Souls howl and scream and cringe. When one tries to run, the others around it hold it in place—or are dragged by the chains connecting them—and one of the Zookeepers comes to punish. These Souls look more humanistic than anything else Jack has seen thus far; they've all been stripped naked and bare the marks of repeated beatings and whippings. Whatever color their skin had been in life, it's all been rendered red or pink since their arrival. Gender is gone, the dangly bits and protrusions already ground into pulp.

Flanking the Zookeepers and their charges are soldiers, or things like soldiers, that may once have been human and are now bright red blights upon Jack's eyes. The red is armor. They've got faces under leathery helmets. They wear bows and quivers on their backs, and some ride black steeds snorting fire and smoke.

They're still getting closer.

The Crewmen build with amazing speed, pulling necessary tools from the lines that function as their bodies, and even fitting bits of themselves, as needed, into the structures they're creating. One splits itself in half so the two can move a particular stone. Their machines, Jack realizes, are just as sketchy, if powerful, and will soon be upon him.

Jack Harlow withdraws the pennies from his pocket, but hesitates when he hears yelling. He sees a group of chained Souls pointing in his direction, and a pair of Souls that have slipped their chains running toward him. The Zookeepers hold back those that are left behind, but the two scramble with all their speed, all their might, and manage to pass the heavy machinery. On ashen ground, they double their efforts. They run for Jack as though he might be their salvation.

Seemingly from nowhere, an arrow pierces one of the Souls in the center of its back. It drops to the ground. Its companion hesitates.

Instantly, one of the soldiers is upon the fallen Soul. He pins it to the ash with a sword. The machinery reaches them a moment later, rolling over the Soul, encasing it in solid burning rock.

Jack steps back. In almost no time at all, the Soul has been made into a living statue, frozen forever in rock just a degree lower than the melting point. He can hear it screaming from inside, though nothing moves.

The second fleeing Soul, halfway between its fallen comrade and the DarkWalker, stops. It turns around, opens its arms wide, and accepts a barrage of arrows.

Jack waits neither to learn its fate nor his own, should he stay, but rubs the pennies together, creating a shower of sparks he can only see because of the gray ash around him, and suddenly there is no ash.

Jack enters another hell.

5.

It's loud. It's bright. Jack squints, and holds up his arm to block the light, but it comes from everywhere. It screeches and scratches, and strikes his ears with sledgehammers. Jack staggers under the weight of it all. None of his senses can focus. There are tastes of crimson in the air, and rusted scents very much like textures, harsh and rough and sharp.

He rubs the pennies till they're raw copper (the color, not the metal) between his fingers, and slips into another hell.

It's quiet. It's dark. Jack drops to his knees—or hangs upside down, it's hard to say. He reaches forward and backwards and finds himself facing a giant, feline eye. It's feral, and easily twice his size. The thing, if it's a thing, if it's more than merely an eye, blinks and says in an absurdly proper British accent, "You look hungry. Or do I mean tasty? Why yes, that's precisely what I mean."

Jack floats in front of the eye, and almost loses the pennies to the weightlessness, but he keeps them and rubs them even as the giant eye blinks again.

He perches on a rocky outcropping on the side of an enormous mountain. The heights reach into miasmic clouds and lightning storms. The depths descend through smoke and shadow and soot and ash. Here, on this outcropping, between one extreme and another, Jack manages to take a full breath. It doesn't scald him. It's a struggle to not look down. It causes vertiginous swaying in his head, if not in his body; he grips the mountain behind him.

The rock is harsh and hot, brittle and crumbly, but it holds. The outcropping is only large enough for him to sit and dangle his legs. Obviously, it's strong enough to support him. He slips the pennies into his pocket. He can at least catch his breath here.

Above, lightning rips through the roiling clouds. Thunder rolls and roils and never ceases.

Something flies toward him. It's small, perhaps the size of a water bottle, and shaped roughly like a woman. He thinks it's a sprite, but it's only something akin to a sprite. He hasn't got a name for it.

She flies toward him rather like a butterfly, flitting up and down and around with apparent randomness until finally she hovers in front of his face. She says, "Who are you?"

"Jack."

She shakes her head. "There's not supposed to be a Jack here. There's not supposed to be an anything here. You're where you don't belong." She shakes her head again. Fairy-like wings sprout from her naked back. Her skin is a pinkish shade of red. Her eyes are oversized for her head, which is no bigger than Jack's thumb, and her breasts are oversized for her body. She has no hair, not exactly, but a flowing mane of something skin-colored and veil-like falling haphazardly from her head in fleshy strands that reach halfway down her back.

"You're right," Jack tells her. "I'm not supposed to be here."

She flutters a little closer, throws an exaggerated wink, and says, "Neither am I."

She darts back. The hair-like strands seem to work in conjunction with her wings. She covers her mouth with a hand. "I told you a secret."

"I won't tell," Jack says.

"I've told you a secret," she says again, darting closer, this time coming dangerously close to hitting him. She lowers her voice to confide, "Now you have to tell me one. It's a law. It's like a law. If it's not a law, it should be."

"A secret?"

"Anything," she says. "It's okay. I won't tell, either."

Before he can stop himself, Jack says, "I'm alive."

It's a mistake. It's a stupid mistake. He should know better. But he's confused, angry, frustrated, in pain, starving, thirsty, exhausted, weak, and befuddled. She's lulled him. Through glamour, perhaps, or deception, or luck alone, she's led him to believe she might be somehow safe.

She grins. She grins widely, broadly, immensely, showing rows and rows of needle teeth, and says, "I thought so." She comes in close, almost nestling at his neck, and bites his throat. He feels the pain of every individual tooth.

He tries to swat her away. She refuses to let go. She digs in, the claws of her hands and feet burrowing into his flesh. Her wings fold close to press her against the side of his head, covering his face and smothering him.

Jack tries, again, to shove her off. She bites again, tearing flesh. He can't see, but he hears the approach of something else, something bigger. He pounds her back, smashing her against his face.

She's close enough to his ear to whisper. "*Delicious.*"

Another hit, and he manages to dislodge her. She crashes into the side of the mountain. He moves just half a step away, and finds no ground beneath him.

She waves and says, "Bye bye."

Jack flails, tries to maintain his balance with one leg still on the outcropping, tries to swing his other back. The sprite-like girl darts toward his face. His balance shifts. He drops.

He reaches into his pocket as he falls, scratches the pennies against each other. They almost don't want to work. They threaten to lose their strength as he plummets through the smoke and ash and shadow. He accidentally kicks the side of the mountain. This removes all the grace from his graceless dive, sends his body into an uncontrolled spin. There's a ground, somewhere, that he's about to hit.

It's snow.

It hurts. He's sure several bones have shattered. He tries to hold onto consciousness, but he's not entirely successful. Through the snow, ice breaks his fall.

He doesn't want to move.

For a long time, he doesn't.

A quick inventory reveals no actual bones broken, despite that they should be. His leg throbs. His nose bleeds. His vision wavers, but there's nothing to see but white. The snow completely covers him. He tries to push himself up, to get his bearings, but it's pointless. Snow drives down on him with a blizzard's intensity. It covers him. It already covers him. However long he's been here, the snow has managed to sneak into his hair and under his fingernails and into the back of his throat.

Jack feels nothing but cold and numb.

Jack sees nothing but shadowy white. Shapes shift and twist in the wind, but never become substantial and never become real.

He climbs to his knees. He trembles with the cold. It casts a blue tint over his skin. He doesn't like it.

When he blinks, the tears in his eyes freeze and, for a moment, capture his eyelids. He's never imagined cold like this. It doesn't bite him. It infects him, it infiltrates and deadens him. Jack's joints are freezing together, fused by the ice within his blood. Every movement hurts more than the last. Another half a minute, he'll be frozen solid, unable to reach the vaudoux's pennies and unable to escape.

The wind eases for only an instant, but it's enough for him to see that he's just one of many, millions perhaps, spread across a field, each of them unmoving, each staring at him, each reaching for him at speeds so unbelievably slow he cannot even see the movement.

He tries to deny this. The effort is wasted. His tongue won't move. His lips crack as they separate. The breath he draws snakes icily into his gut. It hurts as though he'd been stabbed with a iciclic katana.

There's a woman near, blue-tinted skin, hairless, staring directly at him. At first, he thinks she's been frozen into a statue like all the others, but then she tilts her head. She blinks, successfully, twice, making a show of it, each blink sounding like tinkling bells.

She's an Ice Demon. And from all around her, in answer to her call, other bells sound, other Ice Demons blinking, coming closer to examine the new arrival.

She hops to him, reaches with a finger to touch Jack's cheek. He can't even pull back. Her finger is so much colder, so much more deeply frigid, it burns.

She grins an unfriendly, carnivorous grin.

Another, behind him, runs icicle fingers through his hair, scratching his scalp, penetrating his skull with frozen ivy-like tendrils. Jack can barely move. He's nearly frozen solid. Even the pennies are frozen. When he rubs them together, they almost slide away. If he drops one, he'll never be able to retrieve it. He'll never be able to bend to begin the search. He'll never move again.

But he manages to create friction. Friction creates heat. Heat brings another hell.

6.

The hall is narrow and short, ending at a door on one side and a staircase on the other. The walls were once white, but are now dirty and stained by indescribable layers of gunk, blood, feces, and other crap. It's cheap plasterboard; Jack, even weakened, could probably put a fist through it.

The door is just as flimsy, just as white and funky. The stairs are tight, short and steep; they rise to darkness on Jack's left.

His nose is assaulted. He's got a better sense of smell than the average man; all his senses are just a touch more acute. He detects dog, smoke, and roasting meat, which makes him hungry but also frightens him. He suspects he knows what kind of meats is roasting. There's also shit and vomit and other absolutely offensive odors.

Screams resound every direction. The thin walls mute nothing. There's also laughter, and thunderous running, as though entire cavalries ride through these halls, and the whistling of steam through tight pipes.

The door bursts open, and one of those cavalries— sans horses—floods the tiny hall. Some souls crawl on the walls, or on the heads and shoulders of others. They're a lot like people, scarred, bleeding, and burnt, screaming and cackling as they shove their way through. They push into and through Jack as the screaming cavalry mounts the stairs. Some stumble as they run, and others scramble over the fallen. Jack's halfway up the stairs before he realizes he's even moved; he cannot resist the tide.

The stairs lead to another tiny corridor, a T-junction, at which the mob divides and flows in both directions.

One of them, beside Jack now, meets Jack's eyes and opens his mouth more broadly than possible. Teeth appear normal, though most are missing, but the tongue's stunted and scarred on the end. Eyes are wild. He's screaming, without voice, and the force of his breath, brings tears to Jack's eyes.

Then there's another, female, one eye fused shut, the other iris cat-like and green. When she screams, it pierces Jack's ears.

Another tight turn in the labyrinth, another virtually identical corridor, and the mob becomes lemurs leaping into a dark shaft.

Jack Harlow tries to stop, but the momentum carries him over the edge. He's pushed over someone who has fallen, and is then in the air.

It's a short drop. His ankle protests when he lands on someone's arm. A woman falls on top of him, shoving him forward, out of the crashing bodies. The mob moves like a single entity, without thought or reason, taking turns and forcing their way through doorways, constantly stampeding over their own members and collecting others as they move.

A whip cracks up ahead, past a corner so Jack cannot see it. The sound cuts all other sounds. The mob, as an entity, twitches, and finally Jack finds himself stopped.

There's the woman again, looking at him with horror in her one eye. There's another woman, shaking her head and tearing chunks of hair from her own bleeding scalp.

Some of the mob retreats, running into others that are still surging forward. More scatter, climbing through a hole in the ceiling, fleeing down a side hall, no longer a single entity able to draw Jack with it.

The whip sounds again, closer.

"No," the one-eyed woman whimpers; it's the only word he's heard. She turns to flee, running straight into a smaller man pushing forward. She screams at him, grabs him by the head and shoves him aside, ripping his ears off in the process, and vanishes around the last corner.

Another whip snaps in that direction.

The mob has shifted from frenzy to panic, which isn't all that different.

The one-eyed woman is back, clutching Jack's chest as though he were her last salvation. She presses tight against him, trembling, but the eye is steady as it locks its gaze on Jack. She whispers. Jack hears her despite the confusion. "You're *alive.*"

Another whip snap, and a man rounds the corner. He wears jeans and a leather vest over a bare chest, carries a nasty looking pistol as well as the whip, and sports a shining shaved head. The whites of his eyes are blood red. The teeth in his grin are sharpened into makeshift fangs. The letters αγκάθι are tattooed on his chest; it's not something Jack can read.

Behind him, the other whip rounds the corner. Equally muscular and bald, this one sports a goatee and a pair of scars on his face that cross at the left eye. Again, the whites are blood filled. Different shade of jeans, spikes on his leather vest, no word on his chest but a pair of symbols, 刺の, etched into the back of his fist. He cracks the whip against the floor like a lion tamer.

They corral the mob between them, until there's only the one corridor by which they can escape. And they do, almost all of them, though the one-eyed woman tries to hide behind Jack. For his part, he does nothing to try to defend her. He's confused. He's weak. He doesn't trust the sickly dim light and doesn't believe what he thinks he's seeing.

"Hells' Angels?" he mutters.

The cross-scarred Angel is coiling up his whip. "No," he growls, in much the same way you'd expect Christopher Walken to growl. "Angels of Hell."

Jack reaches into his pocket to grab the pennies and transport himself out of here. The pennies are gone.

7.

Jack Harlow stands between the two Angels of Hell. The one-eyed Lost Soul cowers behind him, arm coiled around his chest as though he's some sort of hero. The mob has scattered, those that could. A few try to crawl through the stained linoleum floor.

He must've lost the pennies when the mob swept over him. He's sure of it. He's just not sure how to get back there. Without those pennies, without the vaudoux's magic, he's stuck here, in this particular hell. It's possible one of the crowd had grabbed them. Maybe one of the Lost Souls, one of that mad mob, is now alone in a barren wintry variation of hell, or hanging from the final tree of death, or just out of reach of water.

He knows nothing about Angels in Hell. They're not the same as angels, neither the heavenly nor fallen kind, and they're not likely to ride Harleys.

The Angel who had already spoken steps closer. "Who's the girl?"

"Just another Lost Soul," Jack says. She hisses from behind him, using a forearm to ward off the advancing Angel, still hanging from Jack with the other.

"You would protect her?" the other Angel asks.

Jack's mind runs through a string of curses, none of which are particularly articulate or helpful. The two Angels each stand a head taller than him. Each is half a person broader and pure muscle; the coiled whips now hang from their sides but those vicious guns are still in hand. Jack's not accustomed to being in a position to protect. He's used to observing. He can fight—somewhat—but he knows when the odds are stacked against him. Last time he tried to protect someone, it nearly cost him his life and soul, and it did cost him his love.

Quite inconveniently, he realizes, he's not the type to throw anyone, friend or stranger, to the wolves.

He's weak. He's hungry and nearly dead of thirst and he's still sweating from the heat. It's not so hot as other hells, but humidity hangs stagnantly in the air. He's uncomfortable in more ways than are possible, and suffering more than a few pains.

If he says no, they'll flay the one-eyed woman.

If he says yes, they'll flay him first, then her.

The Angels close the gap. One caresses his whip. The other grins, showing off those self-sharpened teeth. Neither lifts their guns. Weapons are superfluous.

"You're alive," one suddenly says, apparently surprised.

"I can't argue that."

The other leans close, again revealing rancid, rotten breath, and sniffs. "Yes, he's *of the living.*" He says it like a curse. The one-eyed Lost Soul hisses again, scampering to Jack's other side. He feels as though he'll stumble and fall if she's not there to hold him up.

Around them, the other Lost Souls—those who have not escaped—have been trying to sneak away, but now they stop, they stare at Jack Harlow, and they whimper.

"Well, you've spoiled a good hunt," the other tells Jack. He's not happy. To be completely honest, neither is Jack.

Jack tries to show no fear. It's not hard, actually; he's too tired and weak to be afraid. He still feels the feet of the spiders and the Preacher's tiny knives. These cave-like corridors inspire a sense of claustrophobia. He's certain he can wander for days, possibly years, without ever finding a window or a door leading out. But if he shows nothing but confidence, even arrogance, he can bluff his way through anything.

He feels no arrogance and no confidence. Without those pennies, he has no means of escape. He has no weapon. No hope.

"Make them go," the one-eyed woman whines. She doesn't even attempt to whisper.

"She's lost," one of the Angels tells him. "She's nothing to you. She'll drag you into pits of madness from which no man can escape."

"She'll fuck you and poison you, knife and praise and pray to you, and damn you," the other says, "without reason and without thought."

"There's another hundred thousand like her in this Walled City."

"Lost Souls," the other says. "No hope, no real voice, no ambition, no regret."

"*You*," and he licks his lip, "still know regret and reason and purpose. Things that only intensify the horrors you will suffer here."

The Angels look to each other, communicating in some non-verbal way, through gesture or eye movement or mind, and one finally asks, more forcefully this time, "*Do you protect her?*"

Jack takes a breath. It's not a comforting breath, like a sigh outside a bar in Key West. It's not a fortifying breath, like when you see a pair of vampires hanging out by the jukebox and you just want to forget you can see these things. It's just enough air so he can breathe out a single word in response: "Yes."

The answer hangs in the air. The rest of the Walled City seems to pause. The last few of the Lost Souls, showing an unusual degree of bravery, linger at the edges of the corners, curious but ready to run. The one-eyed woman hugs him tighter, a transmutation of desperate clutching to a surge of tentative affection. Even Jack didn't know what he was going to say until the word escaped his lips.

It cannot be retrieved.

8.

For a long while, possibly the entire length of a few small eternities, no one says anything. The Angels of Hell regard Jack Harlow. The Lost Soul behind him attempts to melt into his back and completely disappear.

The regular sounds of this hellish place return: distant and near screaming, running, pounding, thumping, even an off-key violin screeching somewhere too close to them. Every so often, the walls tremble. Someone or something turns a corner, sees the impasse, and retreats.

Jack Harlow said yes. He has no heroic speech with which to follow it, no elaborations to make. Everything he is, whether he knew it before or not, stands bare and exposed before these Angels.

The one with the scars crossing his eye has a twitch in his fingers; they open and close into a fist, one at a time, crushing an imaginary stress ball.

The other, with the fangs and tattoo, wears a perpetual snarl, one side of his lips curled back like a rabid dog's, but he at least has lowered his gun and stopped fingering the whip.

"Fine," Fangs finally says.

Then nothing else, more minutes of silence, until finally Jack can stand it no more. "Now what?"

The Angels exchange a look. Scar closes his eyes, conveying some sort of message, something not too far from surrender, to the other.

"Fine," Fangs says again. He turns abruptly.

The Lost Soul whispers, "You're so brave. So courageous. So strong. Through you, I can see things again, and know things, and understand things.

It's...exquisitely liberating, but also frightening, and dangerous, and horribly sad."

"Move," Scar says, gesturing with his gun for Jack to follow the other Angel.

Jack moves. The Lost Soul crowds next to him, not wanting to be near either the Angel ahead or the Angel behind as they walk. There's nothing provocative about the way she holds him; she feels like a child clinging to an uncle during the fiercest of thunderstorms, as though Jack Harlow, DarkWalker, can somehow protect her.

Maybe he can. He doesn't know. They might simply be walking to his death. But he doesn't think so; even if his usual immunity doesn't work here, the Angels of Hell could have simply struck him down. They're walking, descending stairs and going through doorways and, at one point, climbing through a broken window.

The window is an oddity, yes, but it only opens onto another twisting hall, which leads to another set of stairs. They pass rooms, some with doors shut, and in all cases the inhabitants do their best to not notice, and not be noticed by, the Angels of Hell. Most of these people are not Lost Souls like the running, screaming mob. Some are simply dead and suffering. Some hide. Some piss their dirty pants when they see the Angels of Hell—or when they see Jack Harlow between them.

They keep a good pace. Jack has some difficulty keeping up. He can't imagine why he hasn't already died of starvation or dehydration or diphtheria or consumption or malnutrition or Red Death or fatigue or dreamlessness. His heart should have failed by now, his brain should have stopped putting thoughts together—fresh oxygen is in short supply—and his muscles scream at the abuse. The one-eyed woman helps support him, and pushes so he won't drop too far behind the Angel at the lead. She's driven by fear; she doesn't want to come within the grasp of the Angel behind them.

A second window opens onto what might be an alley, though the alley floor looks like a rooftop and there's a ceiling overhead; it's about as wide and long as a Volkswagen, about three stories tall, occupied only by what appears to be an iron radiator from 1976.

They've made a number of turns, climbed and descended several short staircases, but now they come to the long descent. The stairs are dark, and get darker as they go deeper. The Lost Soul has edged in front of him, maybe to be a stronger support, mainly because it's too tight to walk side-by-side. The Angels seem just barely able to fit without scraping the sides, but Jack's sure they were bigger before.

The bottom of the stairs is illuminated by the same dingy fluorescent lights as the rest of this place. They can go forward or to either side. A few steps further, Fangs opens another door to reveal more stairs. Jack's thighs ache.

More than once, he considers trying to make a run for it. They pass a number of other halls and passageways and doors and rooms and stairs and ladders and flimsy gratings in the floor.

Some rooms are shops, complete with neon signs, though most of these are only partially lit. What they sell, exactly, is a guess at best, most likely a nightmare. *Relief,* one sign reads, but that's rather ambiguous in a place like this. *Lou's.* There's little beyond those doorways to give any clue; mostly, they lead to other doors guarded by demonic bouncers.

Finally, through one last door, they emerge onto a platform that actually feels like a platform, with plenty of room to breathe, though the variety of rancid and rotten scents don't encourage the practice. Those might be subway lines on either side. The concrete walls lean toward the center; they look to have a consistency more akin to chalk, with crumbling bits and concrete powder on the floor.

Present company excepted, no Lost Souls venture so deep into this hell. Stringy demonic rodents, yes. Two additional Angels of Hell, one wearing a similar leather vest, the other bare-chested. A tall, thin thing with more needle-like teeth in its smile than physics ought to allow. A woman clothed in writhing coal-colored souls; her canine teeth are sharp, her black hair an extension of the ever-shifting souls. They snake around her in search of escape. Jack doesn't want to imagine the agony of those nearest that woman's razor-sharp skin.

Scar, stepping up from the rear, announces, "We have a problem."

9.

The Mistress—mistress of what, Jack doesn't ask, not even of his mind—steps closer. The one-eyed Lost Soul cowers behind him, but Jack stands his ground. Confidence is important here. Bravado. If he shows any sign of weakness, they'll take advantage of it for a thousand years, over and over again, until they find another weakness to exploit.

Jack Harlow feels like nothing but a sack of weak. Still, he does not tremble.

"I see no problem," the Mistress says.

The thing with the needle-smile licks his lips and cracks the knuckles of both hands by closing his tiny fists. The demonic rodents scatter, not to flee but to get a better view of whatever might happen next. Jack has no good feelings about it.

No, strike that: he has *one* good feeling. *What problem?*

"He's alive," Fangs says.

Ah, *that* problem. Might not be an issue much longer.

The Mistress bends forward to look into Jack's face. He meets her gaze, but she's not testing his mettle or attempting communication. She's deciding on the spices with which to roast him. When she speaks, it's to the Angel, not to Jack. "Does he suffer?"

"How did he get here?" one of the other Angels asks.

"He can't be allowed to leave," the other says.

Needle-smile licks his lips again. "He *can't* leave." As though permission really didn't matter. "But what's this he's got? A *pet?*" He reaches around Jack, for the Lost Soul. She whimpers, tries to back away, slams into the solid and unyielding mass of Scar.

Fangs says, "He said he'd protect her."

The group of them freeze in the silence. Only the rodents move, and chitter, and perhaps one of them laughs.

"What does he hope to gain?" Needle-smile finally asks. "She's a pet without sense, dumb, frightened, a pack animal without her pack, a piece..." He smiles. "A piece of *flesh*, is that what she is? Has he fucked her?"

The Lost Soul clings to Jack from behind again.

"No."

Needle-smile harrumphs. "Pity."

"Even the prince must obey the rules," Fangs says.

"Damned rules," Needle-smile says.

"Do those rules apply to the living?" Fangs asks.

The Mistress sighs loudly, sending something noxious into Jack's face. He tries not to inhale. "What brings you, a mortal, into this realm of hell?"

"A quest," Needle-smile says. "Always, it's a quest, or it's love, or something stupid like that. You seeking the Great Amulet, the Grail, Sierra Madre gold perhaps, or simply some woman who died in your arms?"

"Ah," the Mistress says. "A woman."

Behind Jack, the Lost Soul flinches as though struck, as though hurt, maybe even betrayed, which is foolish to think but Jack Harlow has no idea how any of these things think.

"Great," Needle-smile says. "There are three million, two hundred thousand and seven souls currently wandering the halls of the Walled City. No, make that three million, two hundred thousand and six." His grin widens. "We just lost one. So, living thing, *Protector of Lost Souls*, now and forever one of the damned, tell me the name of your ladylove. Give me her name, and I will tell you, I will tell you honestly whether she roams these halls. I may even direct you toward her, or her to you, if I am of such a mind after you speak her name."

"I haven't asked you for anything," Jack says.

"Acknowledged," Needle-smile says, nodding. "We are not currently in negotiations. We are at an inquiry."

"Formal?" Fangs asks.

"No, not formal," Needle-smile says quickly. "So, brave and foolish visitor, tell me now, her name, before one of us decides to test the rules and rip open your ribcage."

Jack wants to close his eyes. He wants to step away and think. He wants to wake up and find himself dreaming in the back seat of his Mustang. He wants a great many things he'll never have. He doesn't want to remember what led him here; after what he's suffered since entering that basement, he doesn't know that he'll ever feel pain again.

"Lisa Sparrow," Jack finally says with a mixture of regret, hope, defeat, and defiance.

"Ah, yes," Needle-smile says. His eyes roll up into his head as he thinks. "Yes...yes, there is...no, no, there's a sparrow. A *sparrow*." He looks at the Mistress and demands, "Were you aware of this?"

"An actual sparrow?" she asks, eyes wide.

"Genus passer," Needle-smile says, "Family Passeridae, there's a damned sparrow loose in the Walled City!" He looks down at Jack as he strides toward the stairs. "No Lisa Sparrow has ever entered the Walled City." The two Angels of Hell leave with him. The Mistress merely cocks her head and looks more pointedly at Jack. Scar and Fangs step back, but do not leave. The demonic rodents have scattered; they'd gone at the first mention of the sparrow.

"Did you do this?" she asks.

Jack holds his tongue. This may be a place of lies, but he feels he'll be better off not making such an attempt. Let her think what she will.

"I remember counting sparrows," the Lost Soul suddenly says, hugging close to Jack and speaking over his shoulder. "One for joy. One for joy. Isn't that how it goes? Isn't that how it is? Won't it be a sparrow's feather that brings down the Walled City?"

The Mistress's snarl grows.

"One for joy, the sparrow calls," the Lost Soul says, "and he drops a feather—he, I remember the sparrow is a boy—he drops a feather, down go the walls. I remember. I remember, and you can't take that away from me again. It's *mine*. Mine and no one else's." She hesitates. "Mine," she says again.

The two Angels of Hell, crisscrossed Scar and sharp Fangs, step closer, as if to get between Jack and the Mistress.

"It's a true memory," the Mistress admits, lowering her head.

"Congratulations, young soul," Fangs says, tenderly touching her shoulder. "Do you remember your name?"

"I had a name," she says.

"You have a name."

"I have...my name was...no, *is*, my name is..." She falters, then squeezes Jack's shoulder and lets go. "I am Charlotte White."

"Your name," Fangs says, "is Charlotte White."

Briefly, from within and around her, a white light radiates, a stronger, more vibrant white than this hell offers. She's smiling, she's holding her arms out and looking up and crying. Then she's gone.

Fangs and Scar, together, recite a short Latin prayer. The Mistress scowls. The souls coiling around her, registering and reflecting her agitation, swirl and strain and, ultimately, fail to escape.

"Now," the Mistress says, her grin returning, "what do we do with this living one?"

10.

There's a thing called *Hope*. For a long while, well before he reached his crossroads and entered hell, Jack Harlow had none. Here, in the deepest, darkest, dankest pit of the Walled City, flanked by Angels of Hell, face to face with a sleazy, eerie, potentially deadly Mistress, Jack feels once again the slightest twinge of hope.

A sparrow has infiltrated the Walled City.

A sparrow.

He has to let that sink in for a while. His head tells him it's only coincidence. Another part of him, some deep crevice underneath his mind, suggests it's a ploy to break him, that none of this is real, that the Angels of Hell are setting him up for the hard, final fall.

He also registers the number Needle-Smile said: over three million, but that's well below the number of people who have walked the earth. There must've been billions.

Just how many hells exist? And how many other afterlives? Why hasn't he seen some vision of Paradise? He won't find Lisa in a place like this.

Jack turns to Fangs, tattoo gleaming on his chest. "What will they do to the sparrow?" He knows he's ignoring the Mistress; it's not intentional, per se, but she no longer matters to him. He doesn't wait for an answer. "They'll destroy it."

Fangs shakes his head. "It's really just a sparrow."

"It's alive," Jack says.

"Of course it's alive," Scar says. "There are no sparrows in hell."

"Then how did it get here?"

"How did you get here?"

Jack ignores the question. He turns to the Mistress. "Do you intend to be useful?"

She glares. "I find your insolence...rather intriguing."

"I find your intrigue rather nauseating," Jack says. He turns his attention again to Fangs. "You're not an agent of Hell."

"In a very real way," the Angel says, "I am."

"And in another way," Jack says, "you're not. You're an agent of Hope."

"You're perceptive."

"And you're filled with nothing but deceit."

The Angel nods ascent.

"And you'll do nothing to help me," Jack says. He turns again to the Mistress. "What's the story on the sparrow?"

"That Lost Soul remembered everything well enough," the Mistress says.

"They're going to destroy it."

"Demons are stupid that way."

"And when the first of his feathers hits the ground?"

The Mistress grins, and exclaims, "Boom!"

"Right, boom." He looks at Fangs, but turns instead to Scar. "You knew."

Scar smiles.

"You knew, and you didn't stop them."

"Our brothers went with him," Fangs says, "to ensure nothing stops him."

"You're here to destroy this place."

"No," Fangs said. "Your arrival caused that. We're just...you might say *facilitators.*"

"Great," Jack says. "Facilitate me a way back to the world of the living."

11.

There comes a time when you have to stand up and throw aside your fears—those things that have comforted you since your teenage years, since you first learned there was something to fear in the dark.

For Jack Harlow, it is not the dark itself that frightens him. It's his own place in the night. The mystery of himself. For too many years, he hid from the things he saw, he ignored the night shadows and dark faces, he listened to their jeering and witnessed their feeding. He let the world spin without him. He drove fast, or drank heavily, worked as a day laborer to keep himself fed and stole from the dead when absolutely necessary. He's not proud of some of the things he's done. And he's not proud of some things he didn't do – or didn't do anything about.

But it's not a matter of pride. It's about waking up to the world and becoming what he was meant to be. watcher, wanderer, DarkWalker. Until now, it's a role he's shunned and evaded and eschewed. It's not enough to wear a mask of confidence. He's the DarkWalker. He needs no such masks.

Fangs, one of the great and terrifying Angels of Hell, branded by an ancient word, armed with whip and big nasty pistol, with teeth filed into fangs and stained with blood, one of the torturers and warders of the Walled City of Hell, a creature who knows exactly what it means for a sparrow to fly freely through hell, responds to Jack's words as if to a commanding officer.

"This stairway's on the edge," Fangs says, after leading Jack through several winding tunnels and opening a locked door. "It's a long stair. It circles the entirety of the Walled City, in one aspect or another.

When the Walled City falls—and it will fall, trust me on that—these stairs will also collapse."

"And at the top?" Jack asks.

"A doorway back."

At the start of the stairs, Jack looks back to the giant Angel, down from the few steps he's already climbed, and says, "Thanks."

Fangs growls and shuts the door.

There are a lot of stairs. He climbs. The steps vary in steepness and breadth. They are the same as any of the stairs in this hell, dimly lit by obscured fluorescents, crooked, uneven, endless. There's no handrail. The stained walls do not invite support, and even threaten to crumble at a touch.

As Jack climbs, the sounds of this hell pass through the walls as though they don't exist. He hears screams. Pleading. Crying. Lots of crying, individuals alone and neglected, Lost Souls like Charlotte White. There's tuneless music, and thunderous mobs racing down random corridors. He hears gunshots, the clanging of metal, the screeching of chalkboards, the rattle of rusted feathers. Unseen things crash and tumble and boom, sometimes so close the stairway shudders and threatens to throw him.

The Walled City exists on Jack's left as he climbs. On his right, no sounds penetrate the wall, no windows break it. There are no doors, no other entrances or exits from this stairway. And it is a long, long stair.

After forever, he reaches a platform and makes a sharp left turn. Jack Harlow continues his ascent from the Walled City. It's hard to ignore the voices on the other side of that wall now, but if he doesn't reach the top of these stairs before Needle-smile finds and devours that sparrow, he'll never escape. He doesn't know what waits in the world of the living, but he knows who doesn't wait for him here.

It was foolish to think he could find a single person among infinite souls across infinite hells and heavens—he didn't even manage to see one of those. Is that a sign of something?

He doesn't trust omens, tea leaves, tarot cards, dice, bones, stars, soothsayers, oracles, or prophets. He makes his own future. Or he will, once he knows he's got one.

After another stretch of forever, Jack reaches a second platform, another sharp left, the third side of the stairs. He has to stop, catch his breath, rub the burn out of his thighs and wipe sweat from his eyes. It's as though the wall at his side is all that stands between him and the sun, and it's getting hotter as he ascends.

Something crashes. Something loud. It reverberates up and down the stairs, through the wall, out into whatever surrounds the Walled City and back again. Everything shakes, and then merely trembles, and never again reaches what might be called stillness.

Somewhere in hell, a sparrow dies. Its feathers fall. Needle-smile loses his appetite, but that's no consolation to the three million, two hundred thousand and seven souls trapped within the Walled City. Another hell shall fall, eventually becoming nothing but dust and ash and fodder for the silent spiders.

No rest for the wicked, Jack continues to climb. From within the Walled City, the screams grow louder and more constant, more frantic, no longer merely the cries of agony and pain. There's panic. They're still running in there, but now in every direction at once, as though no one has any doubt as to what will happen next.

The walls will fall, and then the city.

Jack Harlow runs. He uses the walls to pull himself, heedless of what he might be touching. He stumbles, and he trips, and he misses steps. His leg muscles scream and cry like a Lost Soul on the inside.

He wonders if the Angels of Hell are laughing at him now. Did they know how little time he had?

He can picture the scene: Needle-smile coming upon the sparrow, the Angels of Hell standing in doorways to block any exit. The bird perching upon a glassless windowsill, staring into the eyes of one of the Lost Souls, seeking something inside him or her, something like memory, something to release them from what's about to happen. The bird seeing the demon with needle teeth, perhaps wishing it didn't have to be this way, perhaps fearing the pain, perhaps proud of its role or merely content to play its part. Needle-smile cupping the bird within his hands, looking at it, maybe even cooing once or twice, and then popping the still-living bird into his mouth. Chewing. Grinning. Self-satisfied and hugely over-confident. One or more of the feathers spilling from between his teeth, fluttering, floating, falling gently to the floor, and that touch is like a nuclear bomb. The floor cracking. Needle-smile's eyes as wide as his mouth. The Angels of Hell suddenly floating an inch above the floor, touching nothing, witnessing the destruction of another realm.

Jack reaches a third platform. The floors still tremble. Cracks are forming in the walls, tiny random things, bits and pieces falling off in flakes. Nothing major yet. Another full-on tremor, an aftershock, forces Jack to pause. Something huge crashes.

He knows he's been climbing for hours. Could be days. Time's difficult to track in hell. With the death of the sparrow, Jack's the only living thing within the

Walled City. He doesn't know what will happen to the Lost Souls and demonic rodents and the other denizens of the Walled City; he doesn't know what will become of the Angels of Hell, or Needle-smile, or the Mistress. He can't really be sure of what will happen to him. But if he dies in hell, Jack Harlow suspects that what awaits him will not be pleasant.

Finally, after another forever and a bit of eternity and an infinite stretch of time, after Jack's legs and lungs have pushed past the point of no return and no forgiveness, after a thousand flights worth of individual steps, Jack Harlow reaches the door at the top of the stairs.

Everything quivers. Crashes continue to sound behind and below him. The walls, inside and out, continue to crack, though the door remains unmarked, untouched, and unmoved.

Behind him, not very distant at all, a section of the stairs collapses. There's dust, a rush of heat, and inhuman shrieks. A wolf-sized rat stares up at Jack from the new hole, and other shapes move behind it. The dim lights flicker, and some fall dark.

Jack reaches for the doorknob and turns. The door out of hell is locked.

# PART III
# THE ORGANIZATION

1.

Jack had vanished without smoke, without sound, as though he'd simply passed through a door, leaving Naomi and the new arrivals—five men in masks, in uniforms and carrying guns, and one woman without any of that—in the basement.

The woman shoots Naomi a venomous look. "Kill her."

The men lift their guns. Three still stand on the stairs, the other two on either side of the woman. Their masks are Carnival style, white porcelain with a sprinkle of color, a star over one's eye, slashes beneath another's cheek. Their guns are big enough, heavy looking, military-grade weapons designed not just to pierce skin and bone but perhaps concrete, steel, and armor.

Time bends to Naomi's senses. She sidesteps the bullets, almost slipping through time, but it's not a trick she can repeat too frequently.

The men are surprised, so they open fire again.

Naomi is a trickster. She's practiced a great number of illusions and sleights-of-hand. She can chance a color, brighten darkness, extinguish light, and make things that are not there appear to be there. She can step into shadows.

The shadows in this basement are cold, weak and thin, and do little to hide her. A third volley of gunfire is coming. She has no time to think. True magic requires preparations and the gathering of ingredients, the focusing of intent, purposeful breaths, a certain amount of time and exacting precision. She cannot create lightning in an instant or cause the earth to tremble or strike her opponents dead by thought.

The woman's eyes follow Naomi into the shadows. Their veil falls. The woman's aura is similar to Jack's. She's untouchable – repulsive, in a way – determined and dangerous, but lacking Jack's potential.

The men swing their weapons left and right, searching the shadows. The woman points. They bring their weapons to bear on Naomi, even if they cannot see her.

Gray smoke descends from the ceiling. Naomi's stretching her knowledge. Her fingers crackle, sweat breaks out on her brow, her muscles burn under the strain. The smoke tastes of ash. It's thick. It coats the guns, clings to the men and the woman. It shifts as Naomi slides through it.

She's quick. She's up the stairs, behind the men, via another slip of time, another sideways lurch. She feels nauseas, but cannot slow down. She's out the door before they can turn around. Gunfire explodes behind her, but Naomi bursts out of the basement, out of the house, and into open night.

Outside the confines of the basement, she's got a lot more room for movement, and breath, and her talents.

Naomi does not run.

When the first soldier emerges from the house, through the same door she's just left shuddering, she's immediately beside him, a knife more like a needle in one hand. She buries it in his neck before he knows she's there.

It burns, to touch him, to be so close. He's like Jack, like the woman, on a somewhat lesser scale, with no true immunity to the things of night and magic, having only what he's developed through close contact with others who have such talents.

Poison on the blade's edge acts fast. He's seizing up, trembling, frothing at the mouth, swelling at all the joints. He couldn't release his weapon if he wanted. Naomi pushes him back, into the little vestibule, creating an obstacle for his comrades.

There are longer, deeper shadows above ground, thanks to nearby trees and bushes and the sharp rays of the crescent moon. She's half in the shadows, halfway across the backyard, nearly into the empty lot beside the house through which the electrical towers cut, when one of the men gets off another shot.

Naomi propels herself forward and sideways and into shadows, seeking any and every means of escape, but the bullet pierces her back and rips into her belly, low and off-center, with a spray of blood.

For a moment, Naomi's senses betray her. She sees merely white, and pain, and the bullet continuing on its slightly skewed trajectory. She falls sideways. She lands a hundred meters away, in a clearing, beneath a thick cloud of shadow and murk and darkness.

Consciousness slips only momentarily. She's aware of it as it goes, an escape from the pain; it returns with something to dull that pain, to numb or mute it. She doesn't know the extent of the damage, or if the bullet hit anything but flesh, but the fact that the pain has already diminished frightens her.

There are still four armed and masked men behind her, and the woman who commands them.

Naomi draws a pouch from her pocket. It's small, though it holds much. She withdraws a few herbs, a powder, a vial of something that tastes awful. They're getting closer, rushing through the bushes, over the fence, through the overgrown grass that lines the path of electrical towers.

The vial first. It's like copper coating her throat, lining her stomach. She drops the vial while suppressing a cough; they probably hear her anyhow.

The men are nothing, albeit dangerous, potentially fatal, and certainly single-minded. The woman, however, is something else, something very much akin to Jack Harlow, another of those watchers who stalk the shadows themselves. Naomi shudders, even as she sprinkles the herbs around her. Any one defense would hide her from the men.

She's not sure anything will hide her from the woman.

The pain in her gut flares. It throbs and vibrates and slices through her. The bullet's still inside. Silver, not lead. They hadn't known what to expect. That makes her feel just a little better.

Her vision swims. The herbs grow around her, over her. She hasn't even tried to sit up. The movement would attract attention, and potentially cause more damage to her insides. The herbs are brambles now. Within their embrace, Naomi feels nothing but cool salving. It's temporary, a mask more than a healing ointment, but it's enough to keep Naomi's mind on the task at hand.

The vial's vile liquid is having its affect. She barely sees her hands anymore as she fades from sight. The pain's still got her breathing heavily and unevenly, but at least she's not moving much. Thorns armor her. The effort will hinder her healing. But there's no point in quick healing if you're a minute away from a bullet through the skull.

Naomi clutches the powder in her fists. The sweat of her palms makes it a sticky paste, not unlike a roux. The powders tingle. If not for the copper taste already overriding her system, she'd taste copper again, or mercury, something equally as pungent and metallic and slippery. Briefly, the powders itch, then burn; but she's already immunized herself against them long ago.

She's not worried about the men. But if the woman comes close enough, if the woman sniffs her out, Naomi will grab any exposed flesh and send the poisons into the watcher's system. The pain of contact may overwhelm Naomi, may even kill her, but at least she won't die alone.

The watchers, even Jack Harlow, are not immune to all things of the night, just highly resistant, and repulsive, and somehow forgettable. Already, Naomi couldn't tell you what the woman looks like, the color of her eyes or hair, her height or size; she remembers Jack because she's worked on remembering him, studied him for hours in the car, breathed in his exhalations, leaned against him in a Florida bar to test her own limits. She's not exactly one of the night. She's not exactly something different. She's an acolyte, an attendant, a practitioner and disciple, all of that and more, but she's also as human as Jack Harlow.

The men are near. They're spreading out, widening their search. They've lost Naomi's track and her scent. She holds her breath. She sees through the brambles and thorns, which have spread for several yards in every direction and shine in the silver light of the sliver moon.

The men say nothing.

The woman remains out of view, perhaps uninterested in Naomi, perhaps searching by other means or simply confident in her foot soldiers.

The bullet shifts inside her. She nearly cries out, nearly gasps, and nearly loses consciousness again. She cannot cast another spell, cannot send a shadow or a sound, can no longer draw upon the favors in her pouch. She lets her breath out in a slow, quiet sigh. She squeezes tears from her eye to prevent sobbing. The pain has her now, has more control over her body than she does. In a last, desperate effort, Naomi holds onto her senses long enough to see the men silently give up the search and return to the house.

2.

Naomi waits.

She dreams, though she does not risk sleep; she fears she'll never open her eyes again. The dreams are simple and unrealistic, idealized memories of Cité Soleil, of which true memories hold nothing idealistic. She remembers a fire, how warm it was, though it had never been about warmth. There's dirt, and vibrantly colored laundry draped across lines in front of ruined concrete block houses, wash buckets, dirty puddles, rocks, rusted sheets of metal posing as walls, trash. She sees gangs patrolling the shacks, controlling the territory—her brother among them.

She doesn't like to remember her brother. She wants to remember him as supportive and kind and all those things an older brother is supposed to be. But he was brutal, a killer, unrepentant, a rapist and arsonist and, ultimately, dead before the age of twenty.

Naomi floats and dreams and focuses on the pain in her gut, the silver bullet, the hard ground beneath her, the cold in the air—anything, so long as she doesn't slip away. She's not yet ready to go. She has more to do.

Naomi waits for the pain to either take her or recede. She waits for the moon to set. She waits for any semblance of strength. She waits for the DarkWalker to return from whence he went.

She waits, too, for the men in the masks, with their guns, and the woman who leads them. She's there, now, on the edge of Naomi's vision. It's hard to tell if she's real or imagined. Mountains in the distance, those are half-remembered, and the sun and the dirt, but the woman moves with a grace Naomi's flickering visions can neither deny nor retain.

The woman walks right to Naomi, as though she sees the Acolyte lying there, despite that she should be invisible, despite the brambles that have grown up around her.

"Nice set of tricks," the woman says, leaning close. "But I think it's time we use you ourselves."

The men clear the unnatural underbrush. They reveal Naomi and expose her. The coppery taste in her stomach fades and she shimmers into reality.

The woman smiles. Behind their masks, the men may grunt or grin or growl or grumble, but their masks' expressions remain unchanged. It's the woman who cannot be touched, must be ignored, passed, forgotten. So it's the woman Naomi grabs.

Naomi throws everything she's got into the one lunge, forward and upward, off the ground and into the woman's arms, so that Naomi can clench her bare hands. The poison paste in her palms penetrates the woman's skin. Her eyes go wide. Unbelieving. There's pain for both of them now; it shocks Naomi into full alertness.

The woman won't let go. She stares into Naomi's eyes. She wears a twisted, wicked smile as a mask. She says, "Jack will come back." The smile thickens. Gels. She adds, "You'll bring him to us."

One of the men grab Naomi roughly by the waist, jostling the bullet wherever it's decided to rest, reigniting the screeching white pain, and finally the world slips away with Naomi's senses.

3.

Jack Harlow, DarkWalker, recently learned to coax locks into cooperating, or to trick them, or to slip them open whilst they're otherwise occupied, and not even the door out of hell can resist his charms. When he finally pushes it open, he's back in the basement. At first, he doesn't recognize it. It could be anyplace. But it's not; it's his crossroads, the basement where he encountered his first ghost. When he left, untold ages ago, there had been a woman, and armed men in uniforms, and the acolyte, Naomi, whom he'd inadvertently left behind. He returns to the faint scents of blood and sulfur and ozone, and the shimmering echo of a familiar ghost.

"That was interesting," the ghost says.

She looks exactly as she did years ago, which is no surprise. Jack can't, by looking at her, date her death; it might've been a decade or a century ago.

She glimmers.

"What happened?" he asks. "How long have I been gone?"

"It's hard to judge time," she tells him.

"Guess."

"An hour. A day. Not more than that. Less. Perhaps an hour."

"Where did Naomi go?"

"Your girl?"

"Not my girl."

"Your girl," she says, "handled herself rather nicely. I'd keep hold of that one."

"She's not my girl."

"Then what does it matter where she's gone?"

It's a good question, and Jack doesn't know how to verbalize the mixture of responsibility and guilt and curiosity he's experiencing. He feels strong enough, as though the simple act of leaving hell has invigorated him, but he's sure he hasn't been gone for all the months he was there. Indeed, it's hard to pinpoint anything in particular about his journey; it all slides together, mixing, mashing, teasing.

The ghost moves. She doesn't walk, or float; she appears next to Jack in the same moment she leaves where she was. "You've aged."

"It's been a few years."

"You've aged twice. Since you left the second time."

"You were here when we arrived?"

"Where else would I be?"

Another good question. He skips it. "What happened after I left?"

"All sorts of things."

Jack takes a breath. She's not cooperating, but he's also not learning anything, or applying anything he's learned. He's trying to use her as a source of information, but giving nothing in return. "What happened to you?" he asks finally, sitting on the weight lifting bench. "Why do you remain?"

"I don't remain," she says. "I linger."

"Why?"

"It's a nice place."

"You were murdered." It's a guess.

But it's an accurate guess. She disappears and reappears, this time near the stairs, away from him. "That was a long time ago."

"I thought you couldn't judge time," Jack says.

She's directly in front of him again, leaning, eye to eye. "I've been in this house for seventeen years, eight months, twelve days, fourteen hours, twenty minutes, and a few seconds. I do nothing *but* count time."

"The man who killed you..."

"Woman."

"The woman who killed you. Is she still out there?"

"She's dead. She's gone. She went where you went. She, however, did not return."

"Do you expect her?"

"No."

"Then why do you linger?"

"Would you go back to where you just were, if you had a choice?"

"No."

"No," the ghost says. "Neither would I."

"You saw where she went?"

"She shot me," the ghost says. "And my son. Then she came down to this basement, crying, swearing, all sorts of language you don't expect from a lady, nor even a gentleman, and she shot herself."

"I didn't know."

"Nobody knows," the ghost tells him.

"Why not?"

The ghost hesitates. She's not looking at Jack anymore, but at a memory. "My husband cleaned it up."

"All of it?"

"Buried us right here in the basement. All of us."

"That's gruesome."

"It was the right thing to do."

"When she shot herself, when your killer died, you saw where she went?"

"I felt the heat. I smelt the brimstone, the very breath of God and the Devil."

"I think I still smell it," Jack admits.

"That's only what you brought back," she tells him. "You were brave, but stupid. I would never do that."

"There's other places, after death," Jack insists.

"I know."

"You know?"

"Of course I know. I'm dead."

Silence. This time, it's Jack not looking at the ghost. After a while, he asks, "What's your name?"

The ghost shakes her head. "Names are for the past. That's not what you really want to know. Before you, Jack Harlow, whose name I *do* know, no one who came into this basement ever saw me. I floated, aimlessly, watching and listening, experiencing, sometimes touching the man who lived here after me. He never felt it. There was a dog, once, that saw me, but they got rid of it. The dog would play with me. I think the dog's name was Buffy. She was white. Curly tail." She smiles. "That night you came down to the basement, your birthday I believe, all your friends, you brought something else with you. I wanted so badly just to touch you, but I couldn't. I almost couldn't. I did, and I don't regret it, but it hurt. It still hurts. I still feel the touch of you, though I know it's only a dull echo of the pain. That pain you gave me, that's what made me substantial, albeit for so short a time. Your friends saw me because of you. You saw me because of you. You still see me, though I shan't be touching you again. I've had my fun. Perhaps I should move on." She shakes her head. "Your girl, the black girl, she's cute, and I love her accent. She's dangerous and evil, and also good, and I don't know what else."

"Do you know where she is?"

The ghost smiles. "Actually, I *do* want to touch you again."

"Sure," Jack says. "Do you know where Naomi went?"

"No." Then the ghost is suddenly directly in front of him. She leans forward, kisses his lips. Jack feels only a brief, feathery touch. She inhales with the pain and she's gone, a breeze and then nothing, no glimmer, no afterimage, no further sounds.

Jack sighs, softly, and leaves the basement. Outside, there's no sign of Naomi or the "intruders", no sign of the people who reside in the house, nothing. His Mustang waits patiently.

4.


Awareness returns in ragged chunks of pain and weakness. Naomi can barely move. It's an effort to open her eyes, so she reserves her strength. Blood's still seeping from her belly. It oozes more slowly now, but it's too thick, wrong in some way. She's dying.

She still has her pouch. She feels it in her pocket. She cannot move her hands.

She's on something soft. Almost soft. Not dirt or grass. Something artificial. A cushion. It's cramped, though, and the air is tight. Naomi's sprawled on the backseat of a car.

The woman is gone, but not too far. They weren't after her. They want Jack Harlow. She's in the back of his car while he's wherever he is. She might die waiting for him.

The thought makes her smile. She'd never imagined such an unimportant death.

Oh, but she's not done yet. The bullet's still within her, being absorbed into her bloodstream, a silver lining for her crimson. It's a residual magic, something Naomi doesn't even control, like breathing for most people. Like a heart beating. And if her body can still do that, can take care of itself, then perhaps she'll keep breathing through tomorrow and the day after that.

Unless the men with the masks aren't done.

She knows nothing about them. Though she knows of many masks worn by many different types of people, these mean nothing to her. The woman, though, is like Jack, or mostly like Jack, and they clearly work for her.

This isn't good.

Without warning, she feels a presence nearing. It's Jack. She knows without knowing how, without needing to know.

This isn't good, either.

He's at the door. Cold wind snakes in when he opens it. It's good to feel the cold, but it's not good at all. She manages to force her eyes open, if not all the way.

Jack's staring down at her, concerned. He's different. Older. He's not been gone for minutes or hours, but months. Years. She wonders if he found what he sought. She can't help but smile, weak as it may be. She tries to say something, tries to warn him, but the effort's too much. A wave of pain slingshots across her flesh. Her eyes shut on their own.

It's okay. She doesn't need to see him. In her mind, he glows, just as the woman glows, and the woman is coming closer.

"Jack," she says, or thinks she says. It's a wasted word, wasted effort. She adds, with all the force she can muster, which isn't a whole lot: "*Go.*"

5.

Jack Harlow wants to argue with the Acolyte. She'll die if he leaves her. She's bleeding out in the backseat of his car. There's a trail of blood from deeper into the empty lot than he can see; he hadn't noticed it until he was right on top of it. The sliver of moon offers little light, but his eyes are usually better than that. He's not re-adjusted to being out of hell.

His mind's still reeling, too, so it's hard to take what Naomi whispers as a real warning. It's not worth an argument; it's the random flailings of a delusional fit.

He tears part of his shirt off; it's nothing but tatters anyhow, coated with ash and web and soot and pain and brimstone. He knows enough of first aid to stop the bleeding, to put pressure on the wound. He abandons the fabric, though, and instead uses his bare hand.

Naomi flinches. Her eyes pop open.

"I have to stop the bleeding," he tells her.

She squirms under his touch, weakly clenching her fists, gritting her teeth. Is the bullet still inside her? Is it the source of her pain? Or is it that he's the DarkWalker, immune to the things of the night and an irritant to them. He knows his touch burns.

He removes his hand. Naomi settles back; her eyelids flutter and almost close. She says, "The woman..."

"Still here," Jack says, nodding. "I know." He senses her, somewhere not too distant, closer to him that perhaps he would like. With her masked men. It seems like so long since he last saw them.

Jack backs out of the car. He doesn't have a choice. He senses the guns trained on him, tracking his every move. He hears the soft footsteps as the woman approaches.

"You, Jack Harlow," she says, "are a hard man to find."

He turns. "Lizzie?"

She shakes her head. "*Elizabeth.*"

6.

A thousand years ago, a hundred thousand, at the very least two lifetimes ago, Jack Harlow once believed he was normal. Before the night of his birthday, before Marie and the lantern and the ghost that started it all, before the wanderings, before his mother's death, before the dark came to life, Jack Harlow lived in a house in this neighborhood. He hung out with his friends, cut school, ignored his little sister as much as possible, read comic books, watched movies, snuck cigarettes from his father's pack. He was too young to have a future, or aspirations, or much of anything.

One day, when he was maybe fourteen, Jack beat the crap out of a guy. He'd bloodied his hands for the first time. He'd felt rage and humiliation. The guy was Jack's age, three years older than his sister, but he'd convinced her to strip naked in the back of the schoolyard. Laughed about it. Pointed. Threw her underwear on top of the school.

Lizzie stood there, naked, shivering and crying, hugging herself, trying to hide by collapsing into herself. They were out in the open, but the naked ten year old wasn't the center of attention for long.

Jack doesn't remember arriving, or if he'd been there the whole time, or if someone brought him there. All he knows is he pummeled the snot out of the guy. Never learned his name, before or after. Never got in trouble for it, either, though he's certain there were teachers who'd broken up the fight. He'd launched himself at the guy, landed on top of him, swung each fist again and again, head shots all. Teeth flying. Blood spattering.

He remembers his sister behind him. While no one else made a sound, no one could believe what was happening, sweet innocent younger sister Lizzie was yelling, "Beat that fucking cocksucker's face in, Jack! Bash his fucking brains! Rip off his dick and shove it down his goddamn throat!"

The day taught Jack a lesson about himself—and about his little sister.

7.

The last time Jack and Lizzie Harlow were in the same room, it was snowing. Not one of those light fluffy snows, as it had been earlier during the funeral, but a white-out blizzard that had roads closed and half of Long Island under lockdown. Aunts and cousins occupied the living room and had taken over the kitchen. They were upstairs, in their mother's bedroom, their father nowhere to be seen. Typical. They were quiet, not talking, not crying, not acknowledging much of anything.

"You're going," Lizzie said. Not a question, so Jack didn't respond. "You're leaving me now?"

"You don't need me," Jack told her. "I can't help myself. How am I supposed to help you?"

"We're family."

"Tell that to our father."

He was downstairs somewhere, halfway between drunk and out cold. He'd been home for the past three days, more days in a row than any other time Jack remembered, and had somehow managed to find a bottomless bottle of whiskey. "She was a good woman," he'd said at the funeral. "A better wife than I deserved. A better mother than you would believe." In the book of decent eulogies, it wouldn't rate a mention.

"Without mom," Jack added, "the three of us only share a name."

Lizzie was angry. Jack was anxious and afraid. He was new to this whole business of the dark, having seen a total of three ghosts and, at the graveyard that morning, someone that looked and smelled and felt like a kind of vampire.

The vampire wore a long gray coat, almost black, almost dusty, and dark sunglasses. He nodded to Jack, and offered a sort of smile in condolence, then drifted away into the snow.

If he'd been less acutely unsure of what he was experiencing, Jack might've realized he hadn't been the only person to see the vampire.

That night, in the blinding snow, Jack took his mother's Mustang, the only thing she left him, which had been mostly his for four years now anyhow, and left.

JOHN URBANCIK

8.

"You've changed," Elizabeth Harlow tells Jack.

She's changed, too, in less than subtle ways. She's dressed like a cat burglar out of *The Matrix*. Her hair's short now, she's thinner, but she carries more authority. She's no longer his innocent little sister. He says nothing.

"Okay," Lizzie says, "you haven't changed a fucking bit. Why did you come back?"

"I was looking for something."

"So?" Lizzie cocks her hip in a stern, motherly gesture. "Did you find what you were looking for?"

"Not really."

"What the hell does that mean?"

"I found something," Jack admits.

"Yeah, well, all the same, you shouldn't have come back," Lizzie says. Jack's having trouble calling her Elizabeth, despite the differences. It should be easy to separate the woman now from the girl then.

"You'll never guess who wants to see you," Lizzie tells him.

"*Dad.*"

"You suck."

"You're too predictable," Jack tells her. "Even when we were younger, even when you were lashing out at everyone and everything, even when you did all those things no one else thought you could ever do, you never surprised me."

"No," Lizzie says. "I never did."

"What if I don't want to go?"

Lizzie's eyes shift to the backseat of the car. "We let your girlfriend die."

108

Jack glances at the Acolyte. He wouldn't exactly call her a girlfriend, but maybe she's the last and only friend he's got. Maybe she's just along for the ride, the thrill, the *something* the vaudoux suggested.

"There's a lot you don't understand," Lizzie tells him.

She's right. But Jack would never admit that. "You're part of an organization..."

"Not just *any* organization," she says.

"You have soldiers. I get it," Jack says. "I'm not interested."

Lizzie smiles. She always had a cute, dimple-filled smile, just as little sisters were supposed to have. "I don't see how you have much choice."

As one, at some hidden command, the men with guns—is one of them missing?—raise their weapons and aim at Jack's face. Their masks make them impassive. They'd blend into the snow if any were falling.

"Don't make it come to that," Lizzie says. "We're only just around the block. We can walk. You can reminisce, if you'd like, and I'll correct you when you go astray."

"What happened to you?" Jack asked.

"After you left?"

"No," Jack says. "You were always this way. But still, what happened?"

"Let's just say I had a lesson to learn," Lizzie tells Jack. "One of those lessons it would've been nice to have had a big brother around for."

9.

Behind Jack Harlow, through the door he'd left open, other things climb out of the Walled City. Small things, at first – demonic rodents, dwarfish shadows, winged creatures the size of a man's heart. A few Lost Souls, aimless, guideless and guileless, blunder through, and then the soldiers, and eventually something big, something huge, something terrible: a prince.

10.

It's a short, anxiety-filled walk to the house in which Jack and Elizabeth Harlow grew up. It looks pretty much the same, down to the cracks in the driveway, the faded blue paint, and the slightly overgrown lawn, but there are three black sedans and one SUV Jack's never seen before.

Jack's anxiety is as much for himself as for Naomi. She might be dying in the back of his Mustang; and Jack might be about to die in his childhood home. The guns make him think that. And the simple masks. He's not *worried*; if it's his time to die, it's his time. Can't argue with faith. But he's just emerged from a variety of hells and has zero desire to return. There's a lot of afterlife out there, apparently, and a lot more options than he'd imagined. He doesn't want to explore more of them. Not yet. But since the choice won't be his...

Someone opens the front door as they approach. It's another guy in a mask. Cameras track Jack's approach from over the doorway, the top left corner of the house, and the SUV; there might be others. A chain link fence marks the backyard; two large black dogs stare at him. He imagines they're salivating, like hellhounds or some other such beasts, but as far as he can tell they're just dogs. There were never dogs here before.

Their father had always been slightly chaotic – when he was around, which wasn't often. Jack likes to think dear old dad had always been a little crazy. Wild-eyed and frenetic, even spastic, attention deficit to the Nth degree. He did jobs in faraway places and sent back postcards, sometimes unsigned, sometimes without notes; Jack assumed some never made it due to lack of address. When they did have notes, they focused on things like historical artifacts, archeology, mythology, locally brewed beers, governmental conspiracies, hidden treasures, friends he'd made and lost, colleagues disappearing in South American jungles, origami, gargoyles, the shape of snowflakes, dust, ancient civilizations, moon pies. Never were the words associated with the images on the front of the cards. Jack's father might be one of the smartest men on earth, but after a hundred words scribbled on the back of a stained photocopy of the Mona Lisa, dad would be finished and move on to the next thing.

Mom was always the strong one. She kept everything and everyone together, despite that Jack never saw any reason why she should.

All this flashes through his head as he crosses the threshold. The floor plan is the same as it was: foyer at the start and den ahead; stairs on the right leading to living room, kitchen, and dining room; three bedrooms and a bathroom a flight above that. Everything else, however, is different. There's no touch of Jack's mom anymore, her tastes having run to antiques and warm colors. All the old furniture is gone. There's a bench instead of a couch, wood without cushions. The entertainment center, once holding a television and record player and shelves full of videotapes and CDs, has been replaced by a wall of monitors and a pair of computer workstations, at which two of the masked men work. Some screens show static graphics, others live video feeds from outside the house and other places— one is the house with the basement—and others show lines of indecipherable computer code. The walls have been painted white. The dining room appears empty. The den contains a large desk loaded with file folders, stacks of paper, photography equipment, and a long, gleaming sword.

Behind that desk: dad, Jonathon Harlow – balder, leaner, more muscular than Jack remembers – wearing a brilliant smile, holding out his arms to hug his prodigal son. Jack realizes for the first time, Lizzie and dad are both watchers.

Jonathon closes the gap between them when Jack doesn't and briefly puts his arms around him. "So glad you could make it, son."

"I didn't have a choice."

"You always have a choice." He turns his attention to Lizzie. "You said he wasn't alone."

"She's being brought in," Lizzie says. "We had to shoot her."

"Will she die?"

"Perhaps."

"See to it she doesn't," Jonathan says, and then he's back to Jack. "I suppose you have a lot of questions, son. And, after all these years, I suppose I have some answers."

Jack has no old, lingering questions; everything he would ask was born this night. "You were waiting for me?"

"We knew you'd come back," Jonathan says. "Which is good, because now—well, tomorrow—we can abandon this post. It's hard to keep a good secret. Small secrets, yes, of limited scope, but we've long since outgrown that." He talks with his hands, pacing back and forth, with many grand but meaningless gestures as though he's allergic to stillness.

"You sent people with guns."

"Yes, well, of course I had to make sure you'd come," Jonathan says. "They've been in touch with you, haven't they?"

"Who's *they*?"

"The organization. The watchers." Jonathan takes a file off the desk, hands it to Jack. "That wasn't actually a question, son."

The file's labeled *Harlow, Jack*, with a date, the night Lisa died. Inside, there are snapshots of Lisa Sparrow, as well as Nick Hunter, the vampire Jia Li and a few other faces Jack doesn't recognize. There are pages of reports, numerous filings, a Post-It on one page that says *Contact established*.

"They want to bring you in," Jonathan says. "You were rogue, and they were okay with that, they didn't really care. But then something happened, it's all right there in that report, and now they think you're something else. Something more. Not merely a watcher. You've made contact with the dark. And you did so again tonight."

Jack closes the folder. "Stop."

Jonathan stops. "Yes?"

"This isn't new," Jack says. "You've always..." It's the start of a question he never knew to ask.

"Since I was a child. You, too, and your sister. And your mom, God rest her soul."

Jack's not sure he believes what he's hearing. "The night I met the ghost, the night I first saw these things, you...did you know?"

"I've always known, Jack."

"How did this not ever come up at dinner?" Jack asks. "Did you *forget* to tell me something was wrong with me? With *us*?"

"There's nothing wrong," Jonathan says. "Especially not now."

"That's why you travelled."

"That's why *you* travel," Jonathan tells him. "But we, here, we use our gifts for good things."

"*Good?*"

"We're making a difference," Jonathan says. "The organization...they don't see the need. They're not like us, Jack. They won't do anything. They can't. They're crippled by their own fears, their guidelines and procedures, their lack of faith."

Jack interrupts. "You *shot* Naomi."

"Only to get your attention, son," Jonathan says. "*She* is not important. But you are. I had to get to you first, before it was too late, before they reeled you in. They're coming, Jack. They're coming for you. And when they find you, I want to make sure you're ready. I want to make sure you work for us even as you work for them."

"You sound like one of your own conspiracies," Jack says.

"I'm part of their organization," Jonathan says. "So is Lizzie. But the men around us, our employees, our eyes and ears, our sticks and rocks, they're just ours. They're not part of that bigger organization. And just as quickly as we set up here, they'll scatter to the winds. This house, son, is empty now, but it's yours. Come back when you need it. Stay now if you wish. There's a bed upstairs, and I'm sure your..." He takes a moment to find the right word. "I'm sure your lady friend will be fine."

"You shot her," Jack says again.

"She'll live."

"You forced me to come here," Jack says.

Jonathan merely shrugs.

"What, exactly, do you want?"

"Just get inside," Jonathan says, this time stopping his erratic movements and staring straight at Jack for longer than ever in history. "Let them trust you. Be my eyes, son, and my ears, and when it's time, be my arm and my fist."

Jack shakes his head. "You've lost it."

"Don't betray me," Jonathan says. "Blood is strong. But there are other things stronger." He holds up a microchip. "Once this is inside you, we can track you by satellite anywhere in this world, and we can, should our little organization be put into jeopardy, we can and we will release its poison in your bloodstream. Don't worry, though, if it comes to that, son, it'll be a painless death."

Jack doesn't have time to respond before someone behind him, one of the men with the white masks, stabs Jack in the neck with a syringe.

"You'll sleep," Jonathan says, even as Jack's vision starts to blur. "When you wake, you'll be one of us, you and your lady friend."

"And when we need to," Lizzie says, though Jack hadn't noticed her return, "we'll contact you. In the meantime, if you see us in *there*," she spits it out like a curse, "none of this happened. They don't know we exist. They won't, until we're ready to let them know." She grins, or the drugs in the syringe cause her to seem to be grinning. Jack's arms fall to his sides, swaying in out of focus, feeling like giant balloons and mile-long fiber optic wire and lead pipes and tree roots drawn unnaturally to the center of the earth.

The last thing Jack thinks he hears before his senses scatter completely is his father telling someone else, "Get him prepped. And be careful with him. That's my *son*."

11.

Jack Harlow wakes to a blinding sun and a barren room. He's on the carpeted floor, a cheap pillow propped beneath his head, a half dozen bottles of water within arm's reach and a manila envelope just beyond them.

The sun comes through curtain-less windows. There's no furniture whatsoever. There's a small bandage over the inside of his elbow, another on his wrist. Both spots are bruised. His head hurts, his tongue sticks to the roof of his mouth, his lips are cracked, his vision blurry. He opens one of the waters and finishes the bottle in three swallows. Relief is instantaneous, if somewhat insignificant. It gives him enough strength to open and finish a second.

Jack stands. This was once his room. The closet's in the same spot. It's open and empty. Out of this room, there's a hall, two more bedrooms, a bathroom, and stairs down to the living room. He hears nothing, but doesn't trust his ears. He walks as quietly as he can to the bedroom door and grasps the handle. It opens easily.

The hall is empty. The bathroom door is open. Downstairs, he can see all the equipment, and all the masked men, are gone; all that remains is a wooden table and a few chairs that have seen better days. His sister's bedroom door is open; his parents' door, however, is not.

His sister's room is completely empty.

His parents' door is locked. He unlocks it silently. He needs no tools, and virtually no time. The flimsy lock was never meant to keep anyone out. Inside, there's no furniture but the bed his father mentioned, with Naomi lying atop it.

Her eyes open immediately. She stares directly at Jack. She's naked, except for the wound dressing; a lot of that cover her stomach, the white of the gauze a stark contrast to her obsidian skin. Her body is perfect, taut and tight, marred only by old, mangled scars over and across her chest, back, thighs, and genitals.

"Do you intend only to stare?" she asks. Her voice is weak, and more heavily accented. She makes no attempt to cover herself, though she lies on top of a sheet.

"Can you walk?" Jack asks.

"I've been healing," she tells him. It means more than simply recovering. Whatever Jack's father's men did to help, it probably would not have been enough without for the acolyte's magical tendencies.

"They shot you." He still can't believe it. "To get to me."

"You're a dangerous man, Mr. Jack," she says.

"Will you be okay?"

She laughs, though it is a brief and pain-filled sound. "You're not done with me," she tells him. "The vaudoux fulfilled his part of the bargain. You have yet to fulfill yours."

Jack smiles. "What am I meant to show you?"

"I'll know when I see it. Now, if you please, give me my clothes."

Her clothes are folded in a pile on the floor. She swings her feet over the side of the bed, to sit, and could easily reach them herself, though that might mean upsetting the wound beneath the bandages. He hands her everything in a bundle. She checks first for a pouch, which she lays on the bed before standing. Jack leaves her to dress and returns to his room, to the water bottles and that envelope.

He knows it's from his dad.

It's not sealed. Inside, there's a card, Jack's keys for the Mustang and a set for the house, as well as a wad of cash. The bills are small denominations, fives and tens, some singles, so it doesn't amount to much. He doesn't count it. The card is like any of the others his dad used to send while traveling, a sepia-toned photograph of a compass and a sextant over a medieval map of Europe. No real details are visible. Inside, his father scribbled only this: *Close the door, damn fool son of mine.*

"Is that a parting gift?" Naomi asks, appearing at the doorway. She's not quite limping, but she definitely favors one side.

"My father always used to send cards," Jack says. "They sometimes said nothing at all."

Naomi barely reacts, except for a raised eyebrow. "Your *father?*"

"The woman," Jack tells her, "was my sister. Lizzie."

Calmly, as if she were commenting on the weather, Naomi says, "Next time I see your sister, I will kill her."

For the moment, Jack ignores it. He's not sure he won't do the same. But Lizzie's family, and that always makes things complicated.

Thunder shakes the house. An unnatural thunder, especially considering the intensity of sunlight falling through the windows.

12.

Outside, things walk through the sunlight – or slither, scurry, slip, saunter, even stride under the full light of day – things of the darkness, things of a deep and forgotten level of Hell, perhaps Angels and perhaps demons, and creatures that cringe from the sun and creatures that revel in it, drinking it in like a newfound drug, things which no longer have a city to call their own. A sparrow's feather brought the walls down. Residents of that Walled City – now a ruin, a mere stain – are out exploring. And they hunger.

# PART IIII
# HELL ON EARTH

1.

Outside, the street seems to undulate. The lawns, too, and even the houses. A wave of vibration expands outwards from the basement, Jack Harlow's crossroads. At first, what's happening isn't apparent.

Spiders.

Thousands upon thousands of gray spiders, some as small as fingernails, others as big as a fist. Outside his family home, with Naomi behind him and a late afternoon sun shining brightly upon it all, Jack watches the spiders climb over cars, mailboxes, houses. He sees no people, not immediately, until he notices someone through a window across the street. Screaming. Running. Arms flailing and eyes closed.

These aren't typical spiders. There are no house spiders, no black widows, no brown recluses or wandering spiders or golden orbs or tarantulas or jumping spiders or funnel-webs. These are hell-spawn, demonic agents, the same that trampled ceaselessly over forgotten hells to make room for something new.

They spread in all directions. There are easily a hundred thousand of them, maybe more, and they're about to reach Jack's childhood home.

Naomi sprinkles something on the ground, perhaps salt, in a circle around them. She grunts as she does so, suffering still from the gunshot. It's a magic thing, a ring of protection, but Jack understands little about it.

"They can't touch me," Jack tells her. "Not here."

"Nor me," she says. "Best to be sure." He files that; she's no watcher, has no immunity, but demonic spiders from hell cannot hurt her?

The swarm thins as it expands. Over years, perhaps centuries, they might reduce this neighborhood to dust.

They crawl over themselves, moving, appearing to be a single entity with infinite moving parts. They make no effort to penetrate Naomi's circle. Like a river around a rock, they simply break and continue, coming back together on the other side. Only a few press themselves against Naomi's invisible barrier. They skitter along the edges as if it was just another wall.

"These," Naomi says, "were not the cause of that crash."

Jack takes his eyes off the sea of spiders and gazes toward the corner. Behind the spiders, bigger things come, rat-like things with red beady eyes and sniveling snouts and long, razor-sharp whiskers. Around the corner, close to the basement, other things, even bigger, must already have escaped.

*Close the door.* Under his breath, Jack curses. He glances at the window, at the person dancing around the spiders, swatting them, freaking out. But the spiders only crawl over and around. The rodents encircle. He doesn't even see them yet, or if he does he can't process the truer threat. The rodents lunge in, seven or eight at once, impossibly large mouths opening to reveal rows of shark teeth. They tear the poor man's flesh from his bones in small bites, nothing bigger than a thumb. Some strip the skin, some burrow deeply, some rip apart muscle and tissue with barbed claws.

Finally, the man sinks to his knees, and then lower, below the line of the window, which is now streaked with blood.

No one else is visible, though Jack hears screaming. He hears sobbing. He hears the screech of tires and staccato gunshots.

When the rodents reach Jack and Naomi, they snarl and snap, they hiss, they bare fangs and sneer, but the circle stops them. Or Jack's immunity stops them. Or Naomi, hissing back at them, showing a warrior gaze, stops them.

There's another booming crash. It comes from the direction of the basement.

"I can't stay here," Jack says.

"If you break the circle, I can't keep them out," Naomi says. "I can't protect myself."

"Make another circle."

She glowers at him.

"Make one now, smaller, enclosing just you," Jack says. "I'm not in their world anymore. They're in mine."

"What will you do?" Naomi asks.

*Close the door*, Jack wants to say, but in truth he doesn't know how to accomplish that. And what about the things that are already out?

Naomi points. "We've got company."

She's pointing upwards, toward a helicopter. News team. They're taping something, Jack's crossroads perhaps, but they're too far away to see clearly. If the cameraman or pilot wears any expression, distance obscures it.

Jack imagines the report. "All of Ronkonkoma, all of Long Island, overrun by spiders and rodents and..."

And what?

He doesn't want to go back to the house. The idea of swimming upstream, through demonic rodents, through spiders, toward bigger escapees and ultimately to the source, fills Jack with an unnatural sense of repulsion. His immunity, his DarkWalker status, works against him. This is why he never took up vampire hunting, never tried to stop the things he witnessed. Always, his own body resists, his heart, even his soul. But this time, he's responsible. He cannot ignore that. He cannot step aside and allow whatever's coming through (demonic hounds, crazy mindless mobs, Angels of Hell, Needle-Smile and the Mistress, and something else still bigger) to simply enter his world. He has an obligation. A duty.

Jack steps forward, breaking the circle, crushing spiders under his shoes. The rodents back away, cower or flee. But some move around him, toward Naomi, on her knees still fashioning her protective circle. He kicks one. It squeals, bounces off the lawn (or off the backs of spiders and other rodents), and scurries away.

Something hits the helicopter. He didn't see it, but he hears the crash. The windshield shatters. The chopper lists sharply to one side, spinning, the rotors visibly slowing. Something drops from its side, not a person but perhaps a camera or a microphone.

The helicopter disappears from sight.

It crashes like thunder, smashing something, perhaps a house or a tree, sending bits into the air. Silence follows. There's no explosion. Only the scent of death, and the tide of hell-spawn beasts.

2.

Jack strides with purpose, with intention, as though he has either. He doesn't know what he'll do or what he can do or what he'll see. He only knows it's his fault.

The things are getting bigger.

First the spiders, then the rodents, and now hounds come from the house. And miniature people, skin red or charred and flaking. They glare at him. They grin. They lick their lips and bare jagged teeth. Some sizzle under the light of the sun and already a few have crumbled under the daylight, immolating in mid-step. Demons, of a type, mainly weak and pitiable, but a mere prelude of what's to come.

Then there's the mob. Three dozen human-looking creatures, their minds all but useless, lost like Charlotte White. They crawl over each other, crossing the lawn as though still stuck between tight walls. As one, they stop. They stare at Jack Harlow. One howls, several whimper, but a few break out into laughter. Nervous chuckling. Uncertain giggling. Riotous clamor. The mob is breaking apart, their hive mentality already failing outside the Walled City.

Jack's stride does not break. He walks toward them. The mob parts, allowing him to pass. One touches his arm, but pulls her hand away with a hiss. He pauses to look at her. She reminds him of Charlotte. They all do. They're lost, directionless, and ultimately doomed. For them, it's worse to be released to earth. They're not a threat. Jack moves forward.

He rounds the corner, comes into sight of the house, the field, his Mustang. The things pouring forth from the house avoid his car just as they avoid him.

Hounds give way to predators, big cats, hellish jaguars, panthers and tigers, Bastian beasts, South American gods all hungry and vicious and unaffected by the light of day. Though they don't attack Jack, they do not go around him. They are unmoved by his untouchable status, his DarkWalker blood.

Flanked by two jaguars, the Mistress herself walks straight toward Jack Harlow. The soul-clothes around her writhe in agony. Some dissolve into liquid. One or two escape, after however many centuries and eons, only to evaporate into smoke and dust. She smiles, showing sharp teeth. "You've made a mark on Hell," she says. "You'll be forever remembered as a destroyer. There will be songs, and a title, whether you would wear it or no. You are a rare, rare creature indeed, and *I will have you.*" One of the jaguars punctuates her statement with a growl.

"You cannot," Jack says.

"You repel me," the Mistress tells him, circling Jack, touching his cheek with the back of her hand, scratching him with her razor skin. "You burn. You *irritate.* Delicious."

The souls around her expand, as though taking a deep breath, and shift. They move to envelop Jack. They slither around his legs, his arms, across his chest. Each screams, individually, and there are dozens. The collective sound pierces Jack's eardrums. They suffer to touch him, but cannot resist their Mistress' will. They wither. They wilt. They recoil from him, yet pull him closer to the Mistress. At first, Jack doesn't struggle, doesn't believe they can move him.

"You are neither eternal nor invulnerable," the Mistress says. "I can change you. Reshape you. Recreate you."

"Then you would no longer be intrigued."

"Ah, you are deep and layered and very well might amuse me for a century. But of course you're right." She grins, tilts her head, her eyes already seeing some far-off future. "In the end, I'll add what remains of your blackened, twisted soul to my dress."

The souls scream, and pull him closer; amongst the agony, malevolence, and viciousness, some wear expressions of pity. Sorrow.

"This world will be transformed before the prince," the Mistress says. "On your knees, Destroyer of Hells. Serve your Mistress well and I will spare you the worst of the suffering he brings."

The souls force Jack to his knees. He resists, but is not that strong. They curl behind his knees, over his shoulders, dying second deaths as they do so. The number of souls encircling the Mistress never seems to diminish.

She stands over him, looks down, grins broadly.

Jack shakes his head. "No," he says. Nothing more. He flexes his muscles. He pushes against the souls. Grabs and chokes them. His fingers burn through their incorporeal necks. He stops trying to break free and instead focuses on destroying. She'd called him *Destroyer of Hells*. Might as well live up to the title.

When he grabs a soul, it suffers and it dies. They're dying, anyhow, under the light of the sun. But he focuses too intently on the souls. The Mistress strikes him with the back of her fist, sending him sprawling on his back. Blood leaks from his nose and lip. His head rings. The skin of her fist is as sharp as it looks.

"I do not need you to be willing," she says, stepping forward.

She's thrown him out of her souls' grip. For the moment, he's got a complete, free range of motion. Even as he scrambles to his feet, though, her jaguars close in on either side. They're larger than real jaguars, or he doesn't know just how big they can get. They're majestic, red where they should be yellow, with black spots and iridescent eyes. Their teeth are long, sharp, and stained with blood and meat. One opens its mouth wide, displaying those teeth, jungle cat teeth from hell, and snaps it down again. Not a threat. Not a promise. More of a big yawn. Each easily outweighs Jack. They're pure muscle. Pure nightmare.

The Mistress is pissed. "Are you mad?" she cries. "Insane? I offer you escape, even pleasure, my own flesh, for which kings have humiliated themselves, for which godlings have wept. You think I'm meaningless. You're mistaken. I'm Mistress to the Thorny Prince himself. I can melt your flesh. I can steal your senses. I can dissolve every bone in your body to dust and take your soft, pliable body to do with as I please. I can make you beg for the pain of my touch." She's spitting the words, furious, unused to being spurned. But she lowers her voice and adds in a whisper, "I can keep you hidden from the prince."

She's close enough to kiss now. Her breath reeks. Sweat glimmers on her forehead. The razor edges of her skin shimmer. Jack punches her.

It hurts – his knuckles come back bloody – but it feels good. She's thrown backwards, perhaps only an inch, but he's stolen her momentum. The souls around her suddenly break free, all at once, revealing her naked body. She's marked with sores and gaping wounds, deep slashes exposing the organs beneath her chest, all hidden beneath her soul dress.

The souls are drawn back to her. They plunge, as though diving from a great height. They cannot resist, so instead they add their own momentum to the Mistress' will. They weren't merely tormented by her; they tormented her in turn. And now, they shift their shapes, they twist and spiral, they become blades to run her through. They slash, they slice, they cut, they sever.

Some divert, and instead go after Jack. They strike, they burn his flesh and cut into him, then suffer for touching the DarkWalker. They cease to exist. Still others stand, momentarily, to defend Jack, perhaps thankful for being freed, perhaps loyal still to the Mistress and wanting to preserve her prize.

The soul dress envelops the Mistress entirely, consuming her face, her fists, her feet. And then it's over. She's regained control. The souls swarm around her, covering the old, persistent wounds, revealing only fresh blood on her face. There are noticeably fewer souls now, dimmer and weaker, less substantial, deflated and defeated. Their insurgence lasted fewer than ten seconds. And the Mistress – she smiles big, eyes smoldering with hate. She glares at Jack. Briefly touches one of the fresh wounds on her face. She'd had some beauty, before; now she's scarred and bleeding. She says, quite softly, "I wear the wounds of my former lovers with pride."

"You should return to the Walled City," Jack tells her. "Rebuild it, if you must. You are not welcome here."

"*Not welcome?*" She laughs. "You open the door for me, invite me, then challenge me with insolence and ingratitude. And now you spout useless words at me as though they carry meaning? You are merely mortal. You do not understanding *meaning.*"

"I will send you back," Jack tells her.

"You have no power," the Mistress says. "You have no influence. You have no hope."

"I brought a sparrow into hell," Jack reminds her. "The very essence of hope, into the depths of your most hopeless, inhospitable Walled City. And you think *I* underestimate *you*?"

His words cause her to pause. The souls continue dancing about her, perhaps digging a little more deeply. The jaguars look from Jack to the Mistress and back again.

The world rumbles and shakes, the aftereffect of something else. While Jack is occupied with the Mistress, other things climb out of the basement, bigger things, creatures and beasts with names out of legend, minotaurs and basilisks and pythons, griffins, things that have committed *unforgiveable sins*, winged beasts with scaly skin and claws.

The Mistress glances to the house, the basement, Jack Harlow's *crossroads*, and sadly says, "Good luck, then. I do hope to see you again." She means it. Then she walks away.

3.

Jack Harlow turns toward the house. The basement. The crossroads. He wants to ignore the fact that the Mistress is so willing to abandon him, but he cannot. He's not stupid. She leaves to avoid a bigger threat, whatever else may be emerging from that unclosed doorway.

He doesn't have to take a step.

Little things still escape: demonic monkeys, conjoined souls, micro-demons fluttering on bat-like wings. Except for perhaps the Mistress, everything that's come through has, in fact, escaped. In the hellish realms from which they come, they were tortured, agonized, humiliated, made to suffer physically and emotionally and psychologically—some for hundreds of centuries. Many give Jack Harlow, DarkWalker, a wide berth, but some recognize him as their savior and acknowledge him with a nod or a smile—well, a grimace. There are things behind them, bigger things, the punishers and executioners, the lords of Hell, and the aforementioned prince.

Jack saw a demon once. He didn't fight it, but he saw it defeated. He saw the red behemoth forced back into its hell. It had come on the pretense that it wished to recover a prisoner.

Such a prisoner stands before Jack now.

Chains of iron and rust, still hanging from his wrists, plainly show where they've been torn apart. Scars crisscross his naked flesh where he's been cut, stabbed, burned, branded, and skewered. His teeth are filed to points, and have been sharpened by iron and stone. He is no taller than Jack Harlow, but broader by half, a solid mass of muscle. His eyes are wide and wild, but after a moment's frantic swiveling, they lock on Jack. He opens his mouth, but the words he find predate any known language. He points at Jack with an oversized finger, finds another language, something more familiar but beyond Jack's knowledge, and growls in frustration.

"I only know English," Jack says.

"Ugly," the prisoner says.

"Did you want to insult me?"

"I demand a promise." His pointing finger is an accusation. Of what, Jack cannot comprehend.

Jack cocks his head. "A promise?"

"Do not send me back."

Jack considers this a moment. In the shadow of what's coming, the earth trembles, the air quivers, the clouds thicken and darken the sky. He has no other interest, but does he dare make a promise to one of the damned? "I have to close the door."

The prisoner's finger curls back into a threatening fist. "*Promise.*"

The day darkens. The ground gets hotter. The massive prisoner takes a heavy step in Jack's direction and says, again, "Promise." It's a plea.

"Yes, sure," Jack says. "I promise. I won't send you back."

The prisoner smiles. It's almost sweet, if not for the repulsiveness of it. "I will seek my redemption." He drags the chains with him as he walks, his footstep thunderous, and doesn't spare Jack another glance.

From within the basement, a roar emerges, a sound both terrible and horrifying. Every window in the house shatters—also in Jack's Mustang and across the neighborhood as far as Jack can see. It hurts his bones. The asphalt in the street cracks, and the concrete in the driveway. Worms rise to the surface, shriveling and writhing. Birds and squirrels drop from the trees. The sky roils. This is merely the precursor.

It shatters the wall as it emerges, growling, all teeth and more teeth, like a shark with legs and wings. It's the size of a truck, chitinous, its shell layers of misshapen charred skulls. Drool spills from its maw, dissolving the lawn as it hits. Its scorpion tail whips about behind it. It roars again, howls, screeches a desperate sound meant to instill hopelessness, fear, pain, and despair. It paws at the ground, ripping a chunk from the earth. The tail smashes part of the remaining wall. Then it lowers its head and fixes a thousand spidery eyes on Jack Harlow.

For years, Jack has relied upon his immunity to the things of the dark. As a so-called watcher, he can see and recognize the things that bump, chew, and kill in the night – untouched. Ignored and forgotten, at best, or acknowledged but still left alone. Since that first night in the basement, when the ghost put her arm around him and said, "Wasn't that just *grand*," he's seen vampires, ghosts, ghouls, wraiths, zombies, all manner of creature, and often knows, on some instinctual level, exactly what they are. Rarely, but sometimes, he knows their weaknesses. He may know their myths, but slowly he becomes aware of the truths. It's like he has some vast sub-conscious memory from which he pulls information. But all that possible knowledge tells him nothing about the hellhound facing him now. And all that immunity, that compulsion things feel to leave him alone, seems to have no effect.

It doesn't just stare and growl and salivate, its gaze paralyzes Jack Harlow. Its many eyes each seem to take a tiny piece of Jack's soul and twist it. He cannot simply shrug off the pain. Jack has no weapon but confidence, but no degree of confidence can stop teeth as long as his forearm.

There are other demonic things crawling from the basement, tiny, miniscule things by comparison, creatures that don't rate a glance. The hellhound pierces one with its scorpion tail, raises it into the air like a shish-kebob. It devours another whole, swallows without even chewing. Its eyes stay on Jack. A thousand eyes. Jack whimpers. He can't help it. The hound crouches, ready to pounce.

But the hellhound hesitates. It sniffs, and paws the ground, and looks at Jack Harlow with something besides hunger or rage. Something like awe? Curiosity?

Whatever it was, it does not last.

The hellhound raises its head and howls, sending tremors through the earth, rattling the frame of the house and Jack's teeth. Then it leaps. It comes down on Jack.

Pain explodes in his side—his ribs—and his neck twists sharply as he is thrown aside—no, carried to the ground—by the acolyte. She hits him so fast, dragging him from the hellhound's grip, he neither sees nor hears her before the wind is knocked out of him. She takes him to the ground a good ten feet from the hellhound, which shreds the earth and concrete alike.

Naomi moves in odd jerks, spreading salt around them, and black powder. She whispers, "I haven't got magic enough to protect us both."

"It would've killed me," Jack says, surprised.

"It hurts to touch you," Naomi says. "But I can, in fact, touch you."

"It would've killed me," Jack says again, this time with awe.

"You're not as untouchable as you think."

"And your circle?" Jack asks. "Will that protect us?"

"No."

The hellhound shakes its head violently from side to side, then finally locates Jack. It snuffs. Charges.

The magical barrier crackles electrically, but it also bends. Jack can almost see its edges collapsing under the hellhound's onslaught. It seems to know what it's up against, and works continuously on the same spot, weakening it, breaking through. Its hot, rancid breath passes the barrier. Its saliva burns the edges, crisps the grass around them. It raises up and slams its solid forehead against the barrier.

Jack sees the cracks.

"I need to get past it," Jack says. "Inside."

"To do what?"

"Close the door."

She glares at him. "If I had time to prepare something—a day, perhaps two—I could close a door. I don't think we'll be able to get near it."

The hellhound rears back again, a renewed effort, and the barrier shatters. It sounds like breaking glass. The vacuums of power and energy – the shifting flows of positive and negative – implode and explode, throwing Jack, Naomi, and the hellhound in different directions. All of them are briefly stunned. By the time Jack regains his senses of balance and vision, the hellhound is bounding toward him again. One long stride, another, and it's only one away.

Streams of blue and red light explode at the hellhound's side. It lurches away, only for a moment, then goes for the source: the acolyte.

"Fast!" she yells at Jack, twirling her fingers in obscure occult patterns.

Jack runs for the back door of the house. It's not really a door anymore, little more than splinters, but the stairs still lead down. They're pulverized, shards of wood that once could hold a man. They bend and twist under Jack's weight, and break, almost throwing him face first into the concrete basement floor. Something breaks his fall.

Something is the ghost, his ghost, the first he saw. He falls through her, and still hits the floor, but without velocity and without pain. He sees the door now. It's large and growing, a vortex spitting bolts of heat and blinding red light and purified despair. Enough to destroy a mortal man. Enough to devastate hope and courage. Blind and main and kill and damn. But Jack Harlow is a watcher, a DarkWalker, who has spent unknowable time across innumerable hells, has witnessed the creation and destruction of these hells. He is the man that brought a sparrow into the Walled City and triggered its obliteration. He is no longer a mere mortal.

He stands. He faces the vortex. The ghost whispers something comforting, something supportive, but he doesn't hear it. It's impossible for his senses to detect much beyond the boundaries of this portal. Eddies and maelstroms dance across the event horizon of this supernatural pervasion of a black hole. Spiders and jackals and demonic soldiers escape in all directions, their momentum taking them past Jack and out of the basement and even beyond the edges of the town; Lake Ronkonkoma will not face these things alone.

But the vortex is nothing more than a door, which Jack unlocked and opened. He can close it.

He reaches in, finding the lock as easily as any lock. He pushes it shut. There's an audible click.

The wind, the energy, the power—all die in an instant. The planet trembles, the universe shudders—everything Jack has ever known or seen or felt or loved or feared—and then it's quiet.

"You," the ghost of his past says, suddenly next to him, close to his ear, where he can hear her perfectly because there is no other sound for miles, "are *not* worth the effort."

Something pounds on the door. Something large. It's a sonic boom, the pounding, and it reverberates too thoroughly. Jack has closed the door, but not locked it, not properly, not against all the things that have been drawn to it.

The door bursts open. Jack is thrown against the concrete wall. His vision wavers. He missed a heartbeat, awakens before he actually falls. A man steps through. An ordinary man. An ordinary man with a charming smile and a crown of thorns, a silver scepter in one hand, a long, thin sword in the other. An ordinary man wearing what might be princely robes, with fiery hair and eyes, and a stride befitting emperors and gods.

The man glances briefly at Jack, throws him a nod and a smile and even whispers his name, "Jack Harlow," as if making an accounting.

His arrival creates a great void on the other side. It sucks back some of the smaller, closer creatures. A swarm of ghosts—an impossibly thick swarm of phantoms, specters, and revenants—plummet into hell through the vortex. Some scream as they fall. Many scream anyhow. Some wear unmistakable serenity upon their faces. They come from all corners of the earth, through air and earth and water, sliding into the remnants of the Walled City. They nearly pull Jack with them. He reaches in again, to close the door, to close it this time and lock it, to seal it, in ways he didn't know he could manage.

The remaining phantoms dissipate, or bounce back to wherever they'd left, or simply cease to exist. Maybe a few cross to the other side the way they're meant to cross. Jack doesn't pretend to know where they go when they go. He pants, folding over as he tries to catch his breath, and this time he thinks it's done. This doorway to hell has been sealed.

Best, he realizes, if he gets far away. It's his crossroads. There's nothing for him to gain here, but everything to lose. How many thousands of creatures did he just let loose on the earth? Millions? Perhaps some will fail to survive until nightfall. But others will devour souls, end lives, create suffering on unearthly levels, and it's his fault. He turns to the stairs, what's left of them, and slumps against the wall. He hasn't got the strength. He cannot even walk out of this basement.

Jack Harlow closes his eyes. For only a moment...

4.

There's a dream, something brief, something dark. Gardens. Brambles. Roses. Wrought iron fences. Moonlight. Running between hedges, arms extended, slapping the thorns and tearing gashes into his hands. The unmistakable stench of hell. Oversized leaves. Thick, twisting branches, mist, leathery wings flapping overhead. Roots tripping him as he runs. Vines reaching down, grabbing, snatching.

There's a dream, something brief, something sharp. Slicing, slashing, stabbing. Moonlight. Running between stone columns, weapons drawn, slapping the stones and leaving gouges. Long, straight corridors, glassless windows, a thousand silent feet running alongside.

5.

Jack Harlow opens his eyes. It's only been moments. He's still breathing heavily. The air currents are easing. The ghost is gone. She, and a million like her, have been sucked into hell, the remnants of the Walled City perhaps, where they will suffer, and it's Jack's fault.

A million former denizens have escaped, small as spiders, large as—or larger—than hellhounds. The Mistress. Unimaginable creatures. It's all Jack's fault.

He went looking for someone, a lover, perhaps true love or something like it. He cannot touch the feeling anymore. It's lost to him, buried, distorted. She's dead, because of Jack. Again: his fault.

How many others will die, will suffer, will become victims to the things he's released?

Jack cannot pick himself up off the floor. He has no strength, and nothing like hope.

"Mr. Jack," the acolyte says. He didn't hear her approach, didn't notice her arms around him, easing him into a sitting position, until she spoke. She doesn't look good. Though she's got gauze under clothes and over her wound, where his sister's bullet found Naomi's flesh, blood has seeped through. There's a gash in her arm, as well, something new, and the blood of something else on her face and hands. She smells atrocious, or maybe it's the whole world. She grimaces in pain with every motion, and it's his fault. "Jack," she says again. "You are awake." She's not asking a question. "You are alive, and with us, still as human as ever." Not *completely* human, he notices; he wonders if that means anything. "You have things to do, Mr. Jack, now that you've unleashed this."

"Too many," Jack says.

"What, the spiders?" The acolyte snorts. "The dogs? The demons? They'll scatter like wind, like dust, a million strong throughout a planet of billions. They are like nothing, shadows of nothing, and the daylight has destroyed hosts of them."

Indeed, daylight reaches the basement, as there's not much left by way of walls or roof above them.

She snaps her fingers three times in front of his eyes, creating a triangular shape that he follows. "Stay with me, Mr. Jack. Focus."

He catches her hand. "I can see."

"Good." She does not smile, though he thinks she should. "Can you stand?"

"I can."

"Then stand," she says.

"The Mistress is out there."

"Merely a succubus."

"The hellhound."

"Dead."

Jack focuses on Naomi's unnaturally blue eyes. He can imagine a man getting lost in them, but not him, not now. He is impressed. "Really?"

"I have never told you a lie," she says. "I won't start now." She expends effort, and swallows pain, helping Jack to his feet. "I'm not here for lies."

He doesn't ask what she is here for. "You said I have things to do."

"A great many things, I hope," she says. They're climbing the stairs. "First, you must drive."

"Drive?"

The neighborhood is a warzone. Several houses have been badly damaged. Trees have been leveled. The electrical towers, the big ones running through the vacant lots between houses, have been scorched, and one knocked down completely. All the wires are torn. Jack can almost see the freely spilling electricity. Debris litters the streets. There are bodies, human and other. Stains. But there is also life: a child here, crying for its mother; a man staggering from his door, bleeding and in shock; distant sirens coming closer; hushed, muted, and broken fragments of speech. Soon, there'll be rescue workers, firemen, EMTs, police, reporters, neighbors, investigators, onlookers, witnesses, hunters, demons returning, explorers, even his father's *organization.*

"Drive," he says. He feels the keys in his pocket. "Where?"

"Does it matter?"

"No," he admits. "Then what?"

"Hide," Naomi says. "What else can we do?"

"I released something."

"You released a lot of things," she says. "That doesn't make you a villain, so you don't need to be no hero.

"I had a dream," he tells her.

She doesn't answer.

"It was important," Jack says. "Just now. I was out, what, a minute? Two? I don't think it was a regular dream."

"Dreams rarely are."

"What did I release?" he asks. She shakes her head. "You don't want to tell me?"

"I don't know."

"He was strong, whatever he was," Jack says. His breath catches. "He knows my name."

"Names are an important thing, a powerful tool," she tells him. "It is not good, that he knows your name. But perhaps he doesn't care. He doesn't need you. You're the DarkWalker; he cannot harm you."

"I'm not so sure of that."

"You are unique," she says. "But so is he. He'll do whatever it is he's here to do, and someone will deal with him. There are hunters. There are exorcists. There are priests and reverends and magicians. There are archeologists and botanists. There are a thousand people better trained, more capable, and more powerful than you."

He wants to ask, *Only a thousand?*

"We both need healing," she says. "We can heal in hiding. Or we can die in vain."

It's a compelling argument. He's won over. He offers no resistance. He needs her support; he's weak and uncertain, and his head is in a fog. "I can't think," he tells her.

She pulls something from the pouch she keeps in her pocket, puts it between his lips. "Try this." It's bitter. Medicine of any type is always bitter. It revives his head. His eyes find focus. What they focus on is not his Mustang. He and the acolyte stop, and realize quite suddenly they are surrounded by mystic ninja.

# PART V
# PRINCE OF THORNS

## 1.

The ninja move with preternatural speed, as though they aren't human – but they are, or once were, but now they're something more. The ninja move around Jack Harlow and Naomi, shifting in and out of focus, blending into shadows that aren't even there. One steps forward as their Representative. Nothing differentiates him from any of the others. They're clothed exactly as a person growing up with American influenced ninja movies would expect, enveloped in black or gray cloth, only their eyes visible, as if they stole their own image from the imaginings of others.

They bring silence. Whatever sounds might have existed before, they've disappeared. Jack hears only his own heartbeat, which races.

The Representative reaches Jack before he should, puts one hand on Jack's shoulder and another to his mouth, and forces something dry and powdery between Jack's lips. Jack never has a chance to resist. The ninja does the same to Naomi. It stains her dark lips, but she doesn't spit it out. Without judgment, better or worse, Jack swallows the powder. They could've run him through with a sword; he doubts the powder is poison.

"I have just fed you poison," the Representative says. His English is nearly flawless, without accent, but his eyes are definitely Asiatic. He's no taller than Jack, lithe but muscular, and since nothing else is visible his eyes are relentless. "It will cause numbness, first," he adds. "Then you may experience some nausea. That is expected. It will thicken your blood, so it stops flowing from your wounds. It will erase fatigue. It will fortify your muscles, but unnaturally. Without an antidote, you both will die. You, acolyte, in approximately seven hours. Jack Harlow, DarkWalker, will likely last nine, unless your body rejects the poison altogether."

"I always thought if I died by ninja," Jack says, "I wouldn't see you coming."

"You saw," the Representative says, "yet you did nothing to stop me."

"We're surrounded." Jack's always been good at verbalizing the excessively obvious.

"And I don't mean for you to die," the Representative says. He presses two folded envelopes into Jack's hand, closes his fist around them. They're about the size of sugar packets. "The antidote."

Jack slips the packets into his pocket. "What do you want with us?"

"The poison will revive you," the Representative says, "so you may fight."

"You could've slit my throat thirteen times over by now," Jack says. "Who do you want me to fight?"

"The Prince of Thorns."

Jack doesn't respond right away. He feels Naomi tense at his side; she's heard the name before. So has he, though not until recently. "He seemed like an ordinary man."

"Did he touch you?" the Representative asks.

"No."

"Did he say anything to you?" The Representative presses closer. "This is important."

"Important, sure," Jack says. "He said my name."

"Nothing else?"

"Nothing else."

"Your name."

"That's what I said."

The Representative shakes his head. "This is bad."

"Bad, how?"

"How do you feel?"

"Like shit," Jack says. He actually feels better; the poison has already begun its work. "How bad?"

"He met your eyes, then, and said your name," the Representative says.

"He just walked out," Jack says. "Listen, I know he's strong, I know what his leaving Hell did, and I'm responsible for all of that, yes. I'm sorry, I'm really very sorry, but I can't do a fuckin' thing to change it. It's already happened. Tell me what can I do now?"

The Representative leans close, so that when he whispers only Jack can hear him. "You must die, Jack Harlow." He shoves a thin knife between Jack's ribs.

2.

Jack Harlow has no desire to die. He has seen what awaits on the other side and has no wish to return. Pain spreads through his gut, tendrils of agony crawling a bit in this direction, a bit in that direction, as though he's been injected with something.

Moments ago, he and Naomi had been walking together, supporting each other, in constant physical contact. He no longer feels her. He doesn't feel much of anything; the numbing agent of the Representative's poison is quite effective. He only feels the new agony as it shoves deeper through his flesh. It burns. It's cold. It grinds his blood into his bones. He's already falling; no, he's already fallen. He's on the ground, and he starts to feel the asphalt on his cheek. His vision remains clear, but he cannot move his head.

Naomi releases a string of Creole curses, but she's taken down far too easily. One of the other ninja has her face-down against the car, arms pinned behind her back. She struggles, but pathetically, like a child against a monster. She can do nothing. She never has a chance to cast one of her spells.

The Representative kneels besides Jack, removes the gray glove from his hand, and touches Jack's head as though comforting him. "Rest well," he says.

Jack wants to let loose with a string of English curses, but his dry tongue sticks to the roof of his mouth, his lips refuse to part, he hasn't got strength enough to shut his eyelids.

"You have done this world a great wrong," the Representative says, stroking Jack's cheek with the back of a finger. "And now you do it a great service."

Jack wants to scream he's alive. He's in pain, yes, excruciating and spreading pain, but he's not dead. These were ninja. There's no excuse. The blade should've done the job. Jack should've died immediately. There should be no chance for suffering, no lingering, no waiting. A ninja should know the exact point to place the knife. A ninja should move quickly and decisively and leave the target dead—*dead*, not dying.

Jack's so mad, he wants to cry. He wants to close his fists and pound the shit out of the ineffective Representative ninja. He wants to laugh. He wants to ridicule. He wants to put that knife in the ninja's eye.

And quite suddenly, though it should be beyond the realm of possibility, the pain explodes even more powerfully in his gut. He spasms, he writhes, he loses control of his limbs and flails – quite uselessly – in all directions at once.

It's quick. And when it's done, he sees all the ninja circling around him, facing outwards, as if he were some prize they meant to defend.

3.

Death comes slowly to Jack Harlow. Before he slips from consciousness, he bears witness to what must be a great and horrible battle. The ninja fight with mystical athleticism and unnatural speed. The samurai have shadows for faces and shadows for swords. A thousand fight on either side, but Jack's no longer sure what he's seeing is real.

The acolyte explodes into a series of fireworks, red and green and white, occult shapes in the darkening sky. She's gone completely now, a memory, an echo, the last few fading embers. She takes ninja and samurai with her indiscriminately. Jack's not sure who is the realest threat.

The ninja, of course, have poisoned him. He struggles to hold onto that, even as the Representative removes his mask and tells Jack, "I will guide you."

Jack wants to say he doesn't have trust enough to be guided anywhere. But his fear of the Walled City, of the cathedral, of the spiders—all of this is suddenly sharp as the killing edge of the katana. He's not an easily frightened man. He's seen too much, understands too much, knows too much. Maybe that's why he's scared.

The Representative speaks in a whisper. Why does he have no accent? No, why does he have Jack's indistinct accent? Why does he look like he's just arrived from Osaka but sound like he's from Pennsylvania?

The last embers of the acolyte have faded. Samurai and ninja fall on all sides. Blood rises over Jack's body. He doesn't like being on the ground. He doesn't appreciate the Representative's tenderness. The man is his murderer, not a friend.

Death feeds on Jack Harlow's limbs first, plunging them into heavy numbness. He tries to wriggle his fingers, but cannot focus well enough to see if they move. They certainly don't feel responsive. Reality comes apart at the seams. There's mist and fog and clouds. Sounds are distant. The acolyte, Naomi, struggles, though she's already exploded and entirely dissipated. The ninja are so silent, Jack can discern each by their specific absence of sound. The samurai are overwhelming.

Why are there samurai?

The prince arrives. Several princes. Charles, perhaps, or Albert, the Bohemian Prince, a half dozen Arabian Sheikhs, an old, old Japanese man—long dead—known as the Prince of the Stable Door. This last leans close to Jack and whispers. But he speaks in Japanese; even approaching Death, Jack Harlow doesn't understand a word.

No, it's the Prince of Thorns, the Thorny Prince himself, trailing ivy, carrying his scepter, scowling at Jack and at the ninja Representative. Ninja flank him. They break their swords against his iron flesh. They burn from within, smoke wafting from their eyes as the whites turn to char.

Jack Harlow's eyes close of their own accord. He knows none of this is real, not entirely, but none of it is pure imagination. He hears drums, distant drums, a thousand men playing the same steady beat on huge, thunderous operatic war drums. He feels the Prince's thorn-filled vines twisting around him, cutting, trying to drive that staccato rhythm into him. The drums fail to be a heartbeat. Jack Harlow releases one last, uncertain breath, but has no strength to swallow another mouthful.

Death comes slowly to Jack Harlow, but it comes.

4.

The ninja don't merely come quickly, they take control of Naomi's body through the subtlest gestures. A hand on the back of her neck, and she cannot help but look in the direction they want her to look. A barely perceptible squeeze near her shoulder blade causes her knees to buckle. They maneuver her like a marionette.

She's been subjected to such manipulations before. A long time ago. In that obscure period of time after she left Port-au-Prince and before she arrived in the United States. Criminal, runaway, fugitive, she found what she'd been seeking. But there had been tests. Challenges. Obstacles.

So she doesn't resist. She knows when there's no point. She drops to her knees and looks away from Jack Harlow, toward the shadowy figures emerging all around them. They cannot be human. They slip through shadows even in the direct light of the sun. They move with a fluid grace equal to that of the ninja. Equal, but perhaps incomparable. They're something like samurai, but there's nothing of flesh about them. Living shadows, without eyes, without masks, in jet-black armor and elaborate helmets, brandishing swords of pure hellish darkness. At first, they equal the ninja in number. Then they double the ninja. Then they double again.

The ninja are talented warriors. They slip, rather than move, skipping across several meters at a time, striking and retreating, striking and retreating. Endless shuriken fly, simple spikes, handmade stars, shattering the obsidian faces of the samurai. A cascade of arrows rain upon the ninja. When they die, they do so silently.

The opponents know each other well. They've battled before. Perhaps a thousand times before. But the ninja, however cunning, are clearly outnumbered. The samurai double again.

The Representative continues to cradle Jack's dying bodies in his arms. Naomi, still on her knees, doesn't know how long it's been since they've released her; despite that the puppeteer ninja have joined the battle, she finds her muscles uncooperative.

The samurai are not human. Though they die, they are not living. Therefore a magical defense ought to protect her from their weapons. The arrows that land next to her, however, look like wood, sound like wood when they clatter. The weapons are not modern by any means, but they appear to be completely solid. Getting into Jack's Mustang might be her best defense.

But her legs won't straighten, won't hold her, won't obey the simplest demands. Her arms tremble and resist; she cannot reach her pouch. Her fingertips, however, move freely. It's not much, but she paints marks into the air, crafts invisible webs. Nothing so strong as a shield, nothing impenetrable, but the slightest suggestion of a shift in the air might save her life. Her earlier wound bleeds again; the pain keeps her focused. But it drains her.

When the prince comes into view, approaching the battle, unconcerned by the flying weapons, the spears, staffs and swords, the fists and kicks, she cannot help but watch. He strides with regal arrogance. He carries a redundant scepter, and also a long, thin sword. His hair and his eyes are fire. The crown atop his head is nothing like what is depicted upon the head of the Christ, but it is made of thorns. This is no punishment. The thorns glitter like jewels, catching colors and emitting darkness like a prism. They seem almost alive.

Two ninja get close enough to strike, their swords slashing from either side. Both weapons shatter. The assailants burn from within. It's unsettling. But the prince ignores Naomi entirely; all his attention falls upon the Representative ninja and the thing in his hands: Jack Harlow's unbreathing corpse.

"If he dies..." the Prince of Thorns says. The threat trails off.

The Representative lays Jack Harlow's head on the street and, quite solemnly, stands. "You're too late," the Representative tells him.

Something in Naomi cracks. There was no spell, but she breaks free of the mystical ninja bonds. She almost collapses, but in Jack's direction, with a slight, muffled cry. The prince strikes the Representative almost nonchalantly, severs his head with a single slash of his sword. The ninja's body drops in slow motion. The prince finally turns to look at Naomi. He scowls. She's so far beneath him, he doesn't waste words or motion. Instead, he raises his sword and falls upon the ninja.

They're slow in comparison, and weak, and fall easily under the prince's fury. Smoke and dust trail the swinging sword. Bodies pile up behind it. The samurai have backed off entirely, merely creating an arena in which the prince bathes in the blood of his enemies. He howls. Thunder echoes his call. The earth trembles. Lightning shatters the sky. Every footfall cracks the earth.

The headless ninja Representative continues to fall. His body never wants to reach the ground. When it does, it does so with a thud, a thunder of its own. The head rolls in front of Naomi. One eye winks.

When the body hits the ground, so does Naomi. She's free of the ninja's hold. Her limbs are her own again. She crawls toward Jack, careful not to touch the dead ninja lest the poisoned edge of some hidden weapon scrape her skin. She feels for his pulse in Jack's neck. One beat, perhaps, or merely her own. She puts her ear to his mouth, listening for any indication, wanting to feel the slightest bit of air expelled. Maybe it's only the wind. Maybe he's dead. It doesn't hurt to touch him, not anymore, not the slightest prickling burn. She inhales deeply and breathes into his mouth. She finds no reaction. Another breath. Nothing.

"He's dead," the prince says, standing beside her now, the tip of the sword tilted down and dripping blood. He's angry. Flushed with rage. Two dozen dead ninja surround them. A hundred shadowy samurais. Above, the sky has darkened to ash. There's no heat anymore, no warmth. Cold doesn't creep in on Naomi, but assaults her. One ragged breath is normal; the next, a plume in front of her. Where she's from, they know nothing of cold. No one has ever felt cold like this.

The prince still carries the scepter. The sword quivers with anticipation, as if alive with thirst. But the crown seems to have dried some, and the thorns have begun to wither. During the battle, someone had managed to hit him. Once. There's a slash across his face, a small one, a thin red line and a single tear of blood at the end. Realizing this, he touches it with a finger. Tastes it. His eyes widen in awe. Then he smiles. And he laughs. It's a good, hearty, joyful laugh, a sound of victory.

When he's done, he stares at Naomi. She's protecting Jack's corpse with her own body, but she's not strong enough to stand. She's looking up at this prince, feeling disdain and fear and anguish and anger and, above all else, pain. He wipes one bloody edge of his sword alongside his pants, staining the regal purple with red. He says, "Brilliant." She doesn't think he's talking to her, or about her; he's not really looking at her, but at Jack Harlow. It's a long, long minute.

5.

The things Jack Harlow sees are not real. He knows this. It's not hell, or anything like it, but a street in Lake Ronkonkoma, around the corner from where he once lived. How many lifetimes ago? Time has become Silly Putty. His head swims. Two different poisons churn in his blood, but the blood's stopped. There's no movement, no heartbeat, nor a single breath waiting to be taken. It's over. Mostly over. He still hears the sounds of battle, the dying gasps of silent ninja, the fury of soundless shadow samurai, the measured breaths of the Prince of Thorns, the calmness of the Representative, and the ragged, near-death rattle of the acolyte's breath.

Think of her as the acolyte, as a thing rather than a person, not a woman, not someone with a name. If she's Naomi, her inevitable death means more—well, less than his own, which is imminent or already passed. He simply doesn't know.

The Representative is whispering. "I will guide you. I will guide you." Over and over, he says nothing else; because he's dead, he's headless, and only the echo of him remains in Jack's head. The ghost.

But there's another, a more experienced ghost, coiled about the Representative, a man who lived and died twelve hundred years ago. An old man. Armed. The swords at his hip look a lot like the katanas borne by the ninja. Sometimes, he's younger, he's part ninja, he's part assassin and part spy, but he's always a prince.

Jack sees the first battle, thirteen hundred years ago, a field filled with cherry orchards. Yellow leaves drifting to the earth, a ragtag band of mercenaries forcing their enemy back, the corpses of things long-dead stinking up the field. The leaves transform into snow, the tree limbs are bare, and white blankets the dead things and dead soldiers on the field. At the center of it, a doorway is closed, shut and locked, shattered and burned; they scatter its ashes, carry bits to faraway lands, over unimaginable seas, into distant realms of ice and into the volcanic mouths of Polynesian gods, to mountains, to graveyards, to poppy fields and temples and fresh cities rising from the earth as if in a single night.

"It was long, long ago," the old man says, using the Representative's whispery voice and unfamiliar words.

The field becomes a town of tranquility and peace, or so they say, though no one says a word; the town becomes a city; the city becomes Kyoto.

"It didn't start here," the Prince of the Stable Door says. "It didn't end here. It ends today."

"He was here before," Jack says without voice.

"He was here before," the old man admits.

"You sent him back."

"We sent him back."

"You prepared for his return."

"I harnessed the ninja."

"You were waiting for today."

"Yes."

Jack takes a deep inhalation, holds it, and says, "Then why kill me?"

"You think you're dead?" The Representative speaks; the old man drifts in and out of him, around him, around the two of them. "Is that why you will not stand?"

"You poisoned me," Jack says. "You stabbed me."

"With a poisoned blade, yes."

"One poison wasn't enough?"

"The second acts with the first," the Representative says. "To mimic death."

"So I'm not dead?"

"Not yet."

"My heart..."

"May be strong enough." The old man again.

"But we need you," the Representative says.

"We are both dead."

"You are his anchor."

"Yours is the soul he requires to maintain his presence here."

"Your death won't send him back."

"It weakens him."

"What happens if I don't?" Jack asks.

The field-town-city darkens. Buildings and trees wither. Mobs of madmen with spears and torches wander the streets. They yell, they kill, they rape and pillage and devastate. Walls form around them, and around Jack, sick walls, spongy things you would never want to touch, covered with stains and filth. Dingy overhead lights replace the sun and moon and stars. Screams punctuate every other sound, the running feet, the thundering voices, the thuds and crashes, motorcycle whines and a gentle staccato of gunfire.

"You've seen what he brings," the old man says.

"You lived there."

"You survived it."

"You escaped it."

"There will be no further escape."

"He will eliminate the barriers between life and death."

"He'll raise his armies. All his armies."

"He will march across the world spreading death and decay."

"He'll bring torture to the masses, and immortality."

"He intends to overtake the living."

"And then he'll overtake the lower realms."

"And then he will overtake the upper realms."

"Until there is nothing left but one Thorny Prince, one ultimate power in all the universes."

"Until there is breath and life and death and agony and endless games of hope and hopelessness."

"There can be no hope when the Prince of Thorns controls what you can hope for, what you can have, and what you will lose."

The old man drifts closer, sets his insubstantial palm on Jack's chest. "It's too late. He knows you live."

"Brilliant," the Prince of Thorns says. He casts the acolyte aside as though she isn't even there. She's naught but gray embers now, ash in the shape of a woman. She resists, like a kitten resisting an oncoming freight train.

"On your feet." The old man commands it, and Jack obeys.

Simultaneously, the Representative and the old man step into Jack. They're insubstantial, like dust and wind. They crowd Jack's senses. They curl his fists. They sneer at the Prince of Thorns, whom Jack now sees clearly, and in three voices say, "We will un-create you, Prince of Thorns."

The Prince's grin broadens. A single drop of fresh blood stains his cheek; this gives the old man a great sense of relief.

Jack's heart does not beat. He takes no breath. The sweat and blood and tears that he's already spilt evaporate, leaving a sheen of salt on his skin, on his forehead, in the corners of his eyes. The sword in his hand equals, and opposes, the weapon carried by the Prince of Thorns. Essentially, Jack Harlow does not live. The Prince cannot use him to draw strength from the world of the living. The Prince has suffered the barest of wounds; this proves he is vulnerable.

The old man and the Representative suffer inside Jack. He's a DarkWalker, untouchable, safe from the things of night, and they've intruded upon him in the most invasive of ways; they suffer, and without Jack's conscious effort, they will be expelled. But Jack believes them. He feels the darkness emanating from the Prince of Thorns. He sees the dry grass curling and dying under his feet. He feels the thorns as though they are his own crown.

Jack and the Prince of Thorns circle each other, commanding the center of the street, surrounded by a thousand shadow samurai and one acolyte from Haiti. Jack carries a sword that doesn't exist. The Prince holds a sword and his scepter. Jack's body holds three consciousnesses; two work together in perfect, practiced unison. All three feel Jack's natural repulsion.

"I need merely to outlast you," the Prince of Thorns says. "You cannot long survive without oxygen."

Jack says nothing; he'd lose air if he spoke, and the Prince is right about that.

"But you," the prince adds, "are overmatched." He attacks. Swords clash. Both seem surprised that it's not immediately over.

6.

Naomi wipes dirt from her face. She's having trouble breathing, but she's being ignored so she's got time to focus on her broken ribs, the bruises, the blood seeping inside and outside of her. The Prince, though he doesn't consider her a threat, did not toss her aside with merely a leisurely flick of the wrist. She's surprised she's not dead.

When she coughs, there's traces of blood. When she blinks, she realizes there's a chance she'll never see clearly again.

But the things she does see:

The Prince of Thorns, larger now, inflated, bulging with muscles and tinted red with rage; his sword is a living, breathing shadow, much like each of the thousand samurai surrounding them.

The DarkWalker, Jack Harlow, living but not breathing, encompassed by someone else, the ninja, the Representative – and also by another, older, stronger, faster, wiser, much more dangerous. His sword is a living thing, borne of fire and of ice, a contradiction to life itself.

When the swords clash, they do so with the thunder of rock gods. They are a storm, boomers and crashers and shakers and tremblers echoing through dimensions, through hell and earth, through teeth and marrow. There's no wind, except in the wake of their movements; there's no rain; no clouds mar the ashen sky.

A thousand shadowy samurai, perhaps once alive, perhaps not, bare witness. Their weapons are drawn. There will be blood.

Others arrive to witness, too. Agents. Micro-demons. Angels. Lost souls. Wanderers. Dreamers. No one with much intelligence. There's another helicopter, distant and hovering. It's the only thing Naomi recognizes as being of this earth. That and the Mustang, against which she leans. She needs its support. It's unceasingly human, a mechanical beast designed to devour distance and time, a mortal thing which will face its inevitable demise; a thing with a soul of its own.

Finally, she pulls in a real breath, albeit none too deep. She rummages through her pouch. She needs something. She doesn't yet know what.

7.

Jack Harlow believes half of what he sees is unreal; half the rest is delusion, brought on by the mixture of poisons and powders and blood. He believes the sword in his hands is over a thousand years old and has burned every day of its life. He believes the old man and the ninja move through him, and with him, and in him; but eventually, his body will expel them. He is still a DarkWalker. That doesn't means what he used to think it did.

Jack Harlow defends himself with thirteen centuries of ghostly skill. His muscles learn the motions, the steps and the dance.

The Prince of Thorns swings again and again, stabbing, thrusting, slashing, slicing. He feigns this way and that, doubles over, but cannot break through Jack's defense. Not with the sword.

"You're not who you believe you are," the Prince says. Another thrust. Another block.

"Never was," Jack admits. Another slash. Another evasion.

"You're a puny mortal thing," the Prince says. Another cut. Another whiff of air. "I was old before your kind was even imagined."

"We defeated you before," the old man says through Jack's mouth.

"I am patient," the Prince says, then moves in for a quick succession of thrusts and lunges.

It's not easy, defending himself. Jack Harlow's muscles work; they ache and burn and scream. He has no breath, no oxygen. He feels his body stiffening. But the moment Jack breathes, the moment he lives, the Prince of Thorns will use his body to reconnect to the source of his power, some deeply hidden hell Jack would never have been able to visit. Below the Walled City, below the cathedral, below the fresh pavement of a brand new hell, there's a pit from which the Prince of Thorns emerged, from which he draws his power. Without that connection, he can be killed.

But the old man, the Prince of the Stable Door, cannot long maintain his hold over the DarkWalker, even with Jack willing. The Representative uses himself as a buffer of some sort, protecting his progenitor, even as his soul is seared. Soon enough, there'll be nothing left of the modern ninja, and nothing to prevent the same from happening to the old man.

There's a moment to breathe, though Jack does not. He sweats. He should pant. He should be choking on oxygen. The Prince of Thorns grins, readying the sword for another assault.

"Move," the Representative whispers in Jack's head.

Too late, and ultimately futile. The Prince of Thorns points the scepter in Jack's direction. Darkness erupts from its end, striking Jack fully in the chest, swallowing and enveloping him. In his head, all at once, Jack is shown a thousand deaths, a thousand agonies, daggers and nooses and rifles and pitchforks and rocks and hands, all tools for murder. Assassination. Merciless and relentless. Painful, unclean, sloppy deaths. Knives, rust, knuckle dusters, avalanches of coal, hatchets, switchblades, bludgeons. Jack hears the screams, the cries, the whimpers. Briefly, ever so finely, Jack experiences a fraction of their pain.

The Prince of Thorns comes at him again, body and sword moving like a hurricane, unstoppable, nearly invisible with speed. Somehow, his limbs manipulated by the old man, Jack bears this latest onslaught.

The scepter continues to glow.

"How many deaths would you taste?" the Prince asks, every word punctuated by the sword.

"Yours will be enough," Jack says.

The Prince falls back. He glares. He growls. He says, "I shall make you immortal, so that I may destroy you again in the morning, and on the morning after that."

Another funnel of darkness explodes from the scepter. Jack Harlow sees the suicides, the pills, the needles, the bridges, the razors. He buckles under the weight of their despair, their utter hopelessness. In the cathedral in hell, they nurtured the slightest glimmer of hope. But here, none can be found. The circles under their eyes are real, the results of neglect and derision and apathy. Their shattered minds echo through Jack's bones. They know nothing of retreat or surrender. Only release. But the agony of release lingers long after the act.

Finally, the Prince's attacks bring Jack Harlow to his knees. And still he comes, swinging down, down, down onto Jack's raised sword, his meager defense. The ninja in him burns and writhes. The old man grimaces with determination.

Thorny vines curl around Jack's legs, over his torso, reaching for the arm which wields his unearthly weapon. He can't get back to his feet. With every strike, the Prince comes closer and closer to his skull.

The scepter bursts again. Thousands of scenes of abandonment flash before his eyes. Stranded on dessert islands. Lost at sea, storm shattering the vessel, not another living soul on board except the sharks and squids and monsters belowdecks. Locked in a trunk, slowly sinking into the bog, surrounded by only the wet, sticky dark. Tied to a bedpost in a cabin in the woods, raving, ranting, seeing ghosts that aren't real, hearing voices that aren't speaking. Chained to dungeon walls. Fed to the gods of the volcano. Alone on the ice in the long, endless night. Half mangled, still breathing, trapped for days in the wreckage off a coastal highway. A high school cafeteria. Atop the mountain. Under the earth.

Jack can't bear the loneliness.

The Prince raises his sword once more. Jack falters. The old man falters. The ninja dissipates into nothingness. And the acolyte moves.

8.

Everyone ignores Naomi. The shadow samurai have eyes only for their prince. The Prince of Thorns sets all his attention on Jack Harlow, which requires everything Jack's got just to defend himself. It's a losing battle; the prince cuts closer with every strike.

She rummages in her pouch.

She sets protections for herself, things she can do with her fingers, symbols in the air, and ancient words. She draws upon sunlight; though the sun cannot penetrate the ashen sky, it still shines up there. She may capture only the tiniest pinpoint, but any little bit helps. She calls upon starlight, and moonlight, and then the wind.

She draws these things to her, to her left hand. It tingles.

She taps into the shadows. She clutches her fist around a mixture of herbs and powders. She feels very much like the ninja, except that they're all dead and she's been left alone. She rubs a bead of mercury into her palm. It rolls around a bit, then melts into her flesh.

The prince raises his sword for the killing blow.

She slips through the air, skittering across senses, the edge of reality, with even greater speed than she'd used in the basement. This isn't her life alone.

She grabs the scepter.

She explodes the scepter.

She wants damage and destruction, but the thing is far too strong and too old. It spreads its energy in all directions. In direct contact, Naomi sees the things everyone sees.

The shadow samurai see sunlight, blinding sunlight and nothing else. They are mindless.

Jack Harlow sees his past lovers, his former loves, girlfriends, crushes, random women on the street. They curse him. Spit at him. Cut his face with their razor-tipped fingernails. They scratch and claw, bite, scream, accuse. There's the one he lost most recently, Lisa Sparrow, a ghost but not a ghost, barely alive anymore in his mind. His mother scowls. A deaf ghost called Claire. Even Naomi, feline and hissing.

They reject him, each of them, one after the other, all at the same time. They point out his flaws, his failures, his weaknesses. They laugh. They mock. They howl. They punch him in the gut, kick him in the balls, stab his eyes, turn their backs, and stomp away from him en masse. They abandon him, there in the street, this huge, enormous, bigger than life street where he had played as a child. In the woods, there, he had first kissed a girl. Still twelve, she laughs at him now, laughs and marches away. In that Mustang, seeming so far away, he lost his virginity. The girl, forever sixteen, shakes her head sadly and says, "You could've...but no, you couldn't at all, could you?"

Only his mother doesn't walk away. Only his mother stands true, tall, hand on her hip, her expression impossible to read. Finally, she says, "I've seen your death, Jack. A thousand deaths. And in every one, you are alone."

The Prince of Thorns sees fields of flowers and puppy dogs, children playing, running, laughing. He sees cities of silver and ivory flourish and grow. Gleaming marble statues wearing inhuman faces. He sees a court, and a judge complete with white wig and gavel. "Your sentence is served," the judge says, pointing down from his high seat with that sharp, metallic gavel. "You are hereby released to the earth..."

Naomi herself sees her brother, the streets of Cité Soleil in all its harsh, high contrast reality. It's dark. Her footsteps echo in the dirty streets. She's a child again, lost, alone, following her brother. She watches him beat another man senseless. She sees the face of the teenager who murders him, raising that gun, pulling that trigger, grinning that mean, nasty grin and turning the gun onto Naomi. She's small. She can't resist. He rapes her, there on top of her brother's still-warm, still-bleeding corpse. He spits in her face after he finishes, beats her, cuts her, cuts her some more, and leaves her for dead.

The Prince of Thorns yanks the scepter free from Naomi's hands. All its power falls back into itself, bringing the images, the scenes, the emotions with them. She's exhausted, as though she'd just experienced everything again. She's crying. Beneath her bandages, she bleeds. Her ribs reignite in furious anger. Her legs falter. The prince smiles at her. *Smiles.* As though it's a complete victory for him. As though the images he saw didn't in some way shake his core. He's impenetrable, undefeatable, indestructible.

But he's dropped his sword.

Jack thrusts his sword into the Prince's chest.

The Prince grabs Jack by the throat and lifts him into the air. His necrotic touch sends tendrils of gray decay into Jack's flesh.

9.

The Prince of Thorns chokes Jack Harlow. Death oozes from his fingertips, burning, freezing, and numbing Jack simultaneously. Pain shoots through him. He hasn't breathed for so long, and now he can't no matter how hard he tries. His vision wavers.

The Prince of Thorns holds him in the air. Jack's feet dangle uselessly. Yet there's pain on the prince's face. Pain, because he touches Jack Harlow, the DarkWalker, the untouchable watcher of the night.

Jack reaches down, gets his own hand around the prince's throat. He manages to force words up through his throat, around the prince's fingers. "Your grip...is weakening."

A thousand shadow samurai move to interfere, but hesitate. Like most things of the night, they are inclined to avoid the watcher.

The sky brightens as the ash dissipates.

The Prince of Thorns falters. He drops Jack to his feet; Jack, however, cannot stand on his own. The two fall together, each trying to maintain a hold on the other's throat, grimacing, sweating, bleeding.

The earth trembles.

The sky cracks open. Rain pours out of it. Thunder, real thunder, rolls in the distance.

The Prince of Thorns releases Jack's throat and reaches for the hilt sticking out of his chest—the sword of ice and fire.

Jack does not release the prince. The Prince's touch may be necrotic to the living, but the DarkWalker's touch is lethal to the dark.

Life, and death, disappear from the prince's eyes. The irises roll away, revealing black, revealing dust. His flesh dries and crumbles. He's hollow inside, and falls apart. The wind pushes and pulls, but the pieces are so small as to be invisible. Nothing remains of the prince but his scepter, which rolls on the street until it hits the curb behind Jack's Mustang. There's no trace of either the Representative or the Prince of the Stable Door within Jack, but he retains some of their knowledge, some of their skills, some of their strengths.

He crawls toward the scepter. Naomi stares, follows him with her head, but does not move. She's already touched it. He wonders if she'll ever recover.

Before Jack Harlow can test the scepter, the Angel of Hell he'd thought of as Fangs bends at the knee and retrieves it. He turns it over in his hands, examining it. "This is a powerful weapon. Nothing like it should even exist."

"Put it down," Jack says. His voice carries authority, despite that he can neither stand nor see straight. Fangs kneels again, gently places the scepter on the street.

"It wasn't the prince," Jack says. "The power is in that." It's not exactly a question, but Fangs nods. "By rights, it's mine."

"It is."

"You touched it," Jack says. "You're untainted."

"I'm inscrutable," Fangs tells him.

Jack takes a deep breath. It hurts. It's the first air he's taken since he thought he died. His heart slams in his chest, slow, strong, and painful. He flexes the fingers of both fists. He hefts the prince's shadowy sword, struggles to hold its weight, then brings it down on the scepter.

10.

The scepter explodes. The vibrations travel the full length of the sword and into Jack Harlow's arms. The explosion is mostly light, without sound and without concussion, but it's still enough to knock him on his ass. The sword doesn't survive, shattering into fragments that drift this way and that.

Fangs is gone. Other things, those daring enough to witness his battle with the Prince of Thorns, scatter slowly, though a few linger, some with scowls, with teeth, with wicked, hungry smiles. The samurai, without masters, flee, not in fear but with relish. They've never been free. One, catching Jack's eye with his shadow gaze, gives a curt nod before disappearing.

Naomi's on her feet, though she walks to him unsteadily. She's something like an angel. She's smeared with dirt and blood, some of it her own, some of it his. She offers a hand to help him stand.

Jack takes a moment to catch his breath. He doesn't dare close his eyes; consciousness hangs by a thread. Eventually, there'll be police, reporters, on-lookers, people claiming to be witnesses. He wants none of that. He finally takes Naomi's hand; she steadies him as he stands. His arm tingles with numbness.

"We were about to hide," she tells him.

"I think there's less need now," he says.

"I have remedies for your wounds."

"We can't stay at my father's house," Jack says.

"We'll find a place," she says.

He looks at his Mustang. Every window and mirror has been shattered, but the tires appear sound. Perhaps the engine will still turn over. "Can you drive?"

11.

The next morning, Jack Harlow sits on a rocking chair on the wrap-around porch of a secluded house in the Catskills. Feeling has returned to his arms. Bruises have bloomed across his body. He's got gauze and bandages scattered all over. He squints in the light of dawn. The sun comes straight in on him at this angle.

Naomi sits next to him on another rocker. Her eyes are closed, but she's not asleep. He doesn't think she sleeps at all. She's not what Jack first thought; his first instinct is not always correct. That should worry him, but it doesn't. Whatever else that pouch of hers contains, it includes strong whiskey and lemon and honey and a variety of spices, all of which she's mixed in a pot on the gas stove for both of them to drink. It still warms his blood. He doesn't ask what she'd made.

The newspaper has a story about what they're calling "The Ronkonkoma Incident". It includes a lot of inaccuracies, a few blurry pictures, one mention of a black woman in a Mustang, and quotes from zoological and meteorological experts. It's pure guesswork, with no basis in truth. The house with the basement was practically destroyed; it will soon be completely taken down, and his crossroads will cease to exist. He wouldn't go back.

This house is borrowed. The acolyte, Naomi, convinced the man who lived here to leave on an impromptu vacation to Europe. Jack was asleep in the car when that happened.

"Did he know what would happen?" Jack asks.

She doesn't bother asking who. She knows who. "I don't think so."

"But you don't know."

"His mind is his own, Mr. Jack."

"I did release things," Jack says. "The night is darker now, because of me."

"Things would've gained release with or without you."

"Without me," Jack says, "they would not be my responsibility."

"They're not now."

Jack turns to look at her. She remains impassive. He says, "There are things I can do."

"There's nothing you can do," she says. "You're a watcher."

"We both know I'm no mere watcher," Jack says. "Not anymore."

She smiles. She tilts her head and opens her blue eyes. "You never were, Mr. Jack. You're the DarkWalker."

# EPILOGUE

1.

An old red Land Rover maneuvers the mountainous dirt road leading to the temporary private oasis of the DarkWalker and the acolyte. It pulls calmly into the driveway, making no noise, no formal announcement, but also no attempt at stealth. The driver is an average looking man with wire glasses and a crisp, charcoal gray suit. His hair's slicked back, neat and conservative. He looks like a high priced accountant, a man without childish thoughts or imagination.

He approaches the door and knocks.

Jack watches through the window. When he doesn't immediately answer, the visitor—as far as Jack can see, a regular, everyday kind of man—knocks again, then calls out, "We know you're here, Jack Harlow."

"Of course you do," Jack mutters.

Naomi answers the door. She's wrapped in a yellow sari at the hip and wears a big straw hat. She's taller than the visitor, but that doesn't deter him in the least; nor do her bare scars.

"You're the acolyte," he says.

"Is that what you call me?"

"I'm here to see Jack Harlow."

"I know," she says. "I heard you call for him. What if I told you this isn't his house?"

"I know this isn't his house," the visitor says. He doesn't consult a pad or a tablet or anything. "It belongs to a gentleman banker named Jeremy Samuels. He's presently in Europe, enjoying a well-earned but quite unexpected holiday."

Naomi nods. "Well earned, I'm sure."

The visitor grins. His teeth are exceedingly white. "He brokered a deal that may have, quite dramatically, reversed his firm's fortunes and saved them from bankruptcy."

"Good for him," Naomi says.

"Now," the visitor says, "I need to see the DarkWalker."

Jack, standing in the archway alongside the foyer—he has to lean, as he's got a lot of healing still to do, a lot of memory to decompress from his visit to the various hells—says, "What's your name?"

"Lance Turner."

"You have an offer for me?" Jack asks.

"Actually," Lance says, "I do. May I come in?" Naomi still blocks the door, which she hasn't completely opened.

"No."

"No, I can't come in, or no, you don't want to hear my offer?"

"Take your pick."

"We know what happened in Lake Ronkonkoma," Lance says. "And three months ago, you met with one of our agents. About the imp."

Jack's jaw tightens, but he manages to say, "That didn't go well."

"There's nothing I can do to change that," Lance says.

"Who are you, exactly?" Naomi asks.

Lance, now that he's turned his attention to Jack, doesn't look at her, but he answers. "I'm Jack's handler."

"Like a zookeeper?" Naomi asks.

"Not like that at all," Lance says, "though it's not an entirely inaccurate description. Jack—can I call you Jack?"

"Why stop now?"

"Jack," Lance says. "Do I need to explain to you who I represent?"

"The watchers."

"We want you in the fold," Lance says.

"You want to watch me."

"That, too."

"You're surprisingly forthcoming."

"I've no reason to lie."

"Why now?" Jack asks. When Lance doesn't immediately respond, Jack adds, "Why not three months ago, or three years ago, or back when I was seventeen?"

"You've been off the grid," Lance tells him. "You've been quiet. You've been non-intrusive and, frankly, insignificant."

"And now?" Jack asks.

"My superiors," Lance says, as though he has no superiors and few equals, "believe you've become intrusive."

"And significant?" Naomi asks.

Lance glances at her and smiles. "Yes."

"That's the offer?" Jack asks. "You want me to join your merry band of gentlemen?"

Lance smiles. "I think you'll find it's much bigger than that."

"What if I want no part of it?" Jack asks.

"We'll continue to monitor you activities," Lance says. "We'll watch, we'll check you when and if we feel the need, and you'll learn nothing. Or they'll have you killed. It can go either way."

Naomi suddenly leans in and kisses Lance on the lips. It's quick, not overtly sexual, but she's got a glamour she can throw around that way. She lowers her voice to a whisper. "Go back to your people. Tell them he needs to think about it. Come back in a month."

"A month," Lance says, nodding.

"A month," Naomi repeats.

"Right," Lance says. The nodding of his head shifts to a shaking. "I'm sorry, but that's not how it works, acolyte. I'm no watcher, just a handler, but I do have my own protections." He turns back to Jack. "And your friend Nick Hunter needs your help."

# COMING SOON:

# DARKWALKER 3
# THE DEEP CITY

# NOTES AND ACKNOWLEDGMENTS

Thanks to everyone who read *DarkWalker*,
enjoyed it, reviewed it, criticized it,
and threw it across the room.
I promise this will only get stranger.

Special thanks for the continued support of
Mery-et Lescher. None of these happen without you.

Thanks, also, to all my First Readers on all my projects;
the Five Horsemen (Mike, Mikey, Coop, Brian); my
various inspirations; anyone who has ever taught me
anything; the ghost of Edgar Allan Poe; and my Mom.

I have missed people. I always do. I am so sorry.

And as always: Sabine and the Rose Fairy.

# ABOUT THE AUTHOR

John Urbancik was born
on a small island in the northeast
United States called Manhattan
at the dawn of a terrible and terrific decade
and grew up primarily on Long Island,
but he has lived in Florida, Virginia, and Australia.

His first novel, *Sins of Blood and Stone*,
came out in 2002.

*DarkWalker* was originally published
in 2012 as the first of a series.
The rest of the series has remained hidden.
Until now.

John Urbancik also hosts a podcast, InkStains,
based on his writing project of the same name.

www.DarkFluidity.com